Copyright © 2015 Pat Mayer
All rights reserved, including electronic text

ISBN 13: 978-1-60489-150-8, trade paper
ISBN 13: 978-1-60489-151-5, hardcover
ISBN: 1-60489-150-5, trade paper
ISBN: 1-60489-151-3, hardcover
Library of Congress Control Number 2015931657
Printed on acid-free paper.
Printed in the United States of America,
EBSCO Media
Hardcover binding by: Heckman Bindery
Typesetting and page layout: Amanda Nolin, Joe Taylor
Proofreading: Teresa Boykin, Joe Taylor
Cover design: Amanda Nolin

Cover Art: "Big Time" by WB Montgomery
www.williambmontgomery.com

This is a work of fiction:
any resemblance
to persons living or dead is coincidental.

Livingston Press is part of The University of West Alabama,
and thereby has non-profit status.
Donations are tax-deductible:
brothers and sisters, we need 'em.

first edition
6 5 4 3 3 2 1

In memory of

Earnest Tucker Murrill

and

Irma Blanche Teel Murrill

"Four legs good, two legs bad."

–George Orwell
Animal Farm

TWO LEGS, BAD

Table of Contents

1. The Destroyer of Worlds　　　　　　　11

2. Hunger: A Love Story　　　　　　　　23

3. Bear, Part One: Mongrels and Monsters　　39

4. Bear, Part Two: What the Dog Said　　53

5. The Alekhine Defense in Four　　　　71

6. Perpetual Reboot　　　　　　　　　　87

7. Flight Path　　　　　　　　　　　　101

8. The Market Price　　　　　　　　　121

9. An Incident of Gravity　　　　　　　129

10. Little Precious and the Virgin Mary Pie　　139

11. Clara, Part One: Single Familiar Object　　149

12. Clara, Part Two: Last Gleaming　　159

creative talent that goes into the design of combat combustibles. Each military inventor, every battlefield artist, really knew his stuff, but do you know who had the finest mind of all? Robert Oppenheimer, father of the atomic bomb. I admire that guy so much, I really do. It's too bad lung cancer got him, but it was in the cards. Every picture I ever saw of ole Robbie, he was holding a cigarette, nuking himself on the inside. Throughout history, critics have called him a monster, but they don't understand that the real monster was the havoc hiding inside those little atoms. Oppenheimer was just a cool guy with enough nerve to peek inside the atom and look the monster in the eye and coax it out to work its magic.

People in St. Bernard have called me names too, just like they mocked Oppenheimer. You can call me Scout the Trout Man if you want, but please don't call me Tater. I hate when people do that, holding my one big mistake against me. It's never going to end because it's "Tater this" and "Tater that," on and on. Some people never forgive and forget. It's no wonder they call this place Dog Town. Actually, it's just as bad when people are understanding and sympathetic, especially the professionals. Psychobabble and slick, fashionable clichés gush out of them. They say I'm a confused young man with an identity crisis and a dead father, no positive role model, and (I love this one) attention seeking. Ha! Like I'd ever want to call attention to what I do.

When I was a kid, my daffy, drunken mother laughed at counselors and shrinks when they warned her about me. She told them I wasn't so bad and she teased me every time I got into trouble, and made a joke out of it, but I understand why she did it. She had her own indulgent habits, just like Oppenheimer. Every day, she floated far away on a sea of booze, and I guess things must've been funny from a distance.

Maybe I see the world differently because I have such weak eyes. The world has always come at me through two pieces of thick glass on my face. As a kid, I was skinny, teased by bullies, blinking back tears behind my bug-eye lenses. I'd run away and hide, fishing in the St. Bernard River, or sometimes I'd sneak money from Mom's purse and spend all day at the movie theater in town. I've always loved war movies; they're my favorite. All around me I saw boys and girls in the theater, necking in the dark, making disgusting smacking sounds. I knew most guys wanted to make love all the time, but not me. I wanted to make war. I liked those loud on-screen explosions and Technicolor flames. Mostly I loved the whistle of incoming and the impact that came off the screen and whomped through my chest and eardrums. Afterward, there'd be sad classical music and drifting smoke on the screen, soft and titillating as a magic curtain that slowly parted to reveal the devastation and the broken bodies. Sitting in the dark, I thought war sounded like violins and smelled like buttered popcorn and Junior Mints.

My first serious brush with the courts happened when I was still a kid. I want to pause here and say that most of my mistakes were made in the interest of science. When I was twelve years old, I decided to find a more efficient way to catch fish besides one at a time with a rod and reel, so I borrowed a stick of dynamite and a fuse from a construction site and ignited it in the river. It threw up a huge plume, but water is very forgiving. It holds no wounds or scars. Only a minute later there was no trace of the explosion except choppy waves and a lot of dead fish popping to the surface. I'd been correct, it was a more efficient way to fish, but the best part of my experiment happened underwater, out of sight. I thought the method was completely unsatisfying.

I barely had time to walk home before Dog Town cops came knocking. They gave me a truckload of crap and I realized that I'd have to do better next time. If I was going to deal with this much bullshit, I wanted to make it worth my while, so I decided to take it to the next level and make a real bomb. For this, I needed the advice of an expert, my mom's boyfriend, Dudley. Dud was pretty cool. He lived in a trailer and he was nice, even though he lied a lot. Nobody's perfect.

Every Sunday, Dud pulled into our driveway in a white Pontiac so gigantic it looked like a cumulus cloud with curb feelers. He claimed to be a veteran of Vietnam, but that was a lie. He actually worked in a BX in Virginia Beach. I know, because I did the math. The war was over by the time he joined, but that didn't stop him from stuffing my head with war stories that never happened. He was in the habit of balling my mom on Sunday afternoons. The three of us would eat lunch, and then Dud and I would take our desserts out on the porch while mom did dishes. I'd blink through my thick glasses and fork coconut cake into my mouth and listen while he told me about exquisite instruments of warfare.

"Now you take your catty-pult," he'd say, "it's a thang of beauty. Fling rocks and fire balls. You can take tires off'n the trucks and set em afire and fling em."

I pictured truck tires arcing through the air like giant flaming donuts.

"Bitchin'!" I said.

He continued, "Then there's bat-trin rams. They're good, but if you want to win a war, you got to use explosives."

"Is it hard to build a bomb?" I asked.

"Heck, no," Dud grinned. "You can make a bum out of anythang."

"Like what?" I asked through a mouthful of cake.

That's when Mom stuck her head out the door to call him inside. As usual, she gave me money. "Scout, walk down to the store and get yourself a treat," she said, like I didn't know why they were getting rid of me. Dud stood up and whispered, "Boy, before next Sunday, you get a couple of fat taters and a can a gasoline and I'll teach ya how to stir up some tater grenades."

Potato grenades? I gaped at him as I backed down the steps with my fist full of coins. Potato grenades! Yes! My little heart bumped in my chest like a bird trying to get out of a cage. My brain skittered, itemizing details of Dud's larcenous plot.

First of all, the gasoline would be easy; there was a can in the garage, but I'd have to secure potatoes and hide them in my sock drawer. Oddly, this held a twisted appeal. It was, after all, a covert operation. Dud and I would be like two combat operatives living off the land, as he said, using whatever we could find to work our tricks.

The next day, Monday, I went to Piggly Wiggly and fingered several potatoes, selecting two that were firm and round like grenades.

I could've paid for them, but that seemed like cheating because it was too conspicuous. Spies don't walk into stores and buy their supplies. I looked around to be sure I wasn't being watched, then I slipped the potatoes under my shirt and ran out the sliding doors like a dog to his dinner. I hid the spuds in my sock drawer and checked on them all week. They were always there, under my argyles. After the potatoes were secured, there was nothing else to do except check my sock drawer, shake the gasoline can, and wait.

At last, when I was nearly exploding, Sunday morning came. I woke up and dressed, clumsy with nervousness, while the minute hand crept around the clock in its monotonous circle. Then it was finally ten o'clock, and then a grinding eleven. I'd been checking my sock drawer and shaking the gasoline can every half hour. At last it was noon and Dud pulled his enormous Pontiac into the driveway. I rushed his car, dancing and leaping like a Jack Russell Terrier. "Forget it, Scout," said Dud, rolling from behind the wheel. "Yer ma found out."

My ribs instantly compressed and squeezed all the blood from my heart and left it empty and quivering. I was lightheaded, so I leaned against his car. My legs still supported me by some little miracle of grit and gristle.

"Found out?" I whispered, "But how?"

"Well, she wanted to know how we was gettin along, you and me, and I mighta let our little plan slip a wee bit. You know, pillow talk and all."

He hiked his britches around his huge belly, turned his back to me, and went into the house. I watched him go, and when the door shut behind him, I spun on legs that felt like jelly and ran stiff-backed to the river. At water's edge, I sat with my arms locked around my knees and sobbed until I was exhausted. Then I rested my cheek on my knees and watched the current flow, slow and steady, unconcerned with mankind's petty disappointments. The river worked its usual kindness and I was calmer by that time, able to think logically.

No question, I'd carry on without Dud and make the grenades by myself. Why not? I had two potatoes, just like Oppenheimer had two bombs. Maybe two was a combustible number. Oppenheimer's two bombs were called Fat Man and Little Boy. It was like Dud and me, a fat man and a little boy. That was no coincidence; it was meant to be. I was getting a green light from destiny.

When the details were worked out in my head, I left the river and walked back home and waited until Mama went to sleep that night. When she was full of sherry and snoring in front of the TV, I gathered my supplies in the driveway. I poured gas on the potatoes and lobbed one into the street, but it only broke apart and never ignited at all. I set fire to the other one, but it didn't explode. It simply burned and made a terrible stink. I went inside and climbed into bed, smelling of gasoline, burnt starch, and failure.

I folded my hands behind my head and took stock of my situation. Dud had said that he'd help me, but it had been a lie. You can't lie to a little kid without causing damage; all the shrinks say it. You can't break your word and then wrap yourself in your adulthood and brush the kid off like an annoying bug. Bad things happen to big mouths.

A few days later, a mysterious fire destroyed Dud's house trailer while he was at work, so he wasn't hurt, but all his stuff burned up. After that, he acted funny and it seemed to be harder for him to come over to see Mama. He always made an excuse until he just quit showing up, so Mama and I decided to take in a movie every Sunday. You see, an event that was unlucky for one guy was an opportunity for another guy. I've always believed in looking on the sunny side.

IT'S SURPRISING HOW many empty buildings are in St. Bernard. It might be a condemned house in an abandoned neighborhood, or a neglected mansion, and maybe two empty house trailers, a dry peeling barn, some sleazy storefronts, and a whole forsaken strip mall with a tar paper roof. Tar paper burns good. There are a lot of empty gas stations, too, and one gas station that wasn't empty, but the owner was an old bastard who hated kids and watched them like they were going to steal something and growled and said to go home to their crazy drunk mama.

When his station blew up, the timing was perfect. The underground tanks had just been refilled. A joyful ignition came to pass deep in the ground and the whole street bucked in a rolling ripple and burst open like a roaring wound. People heard the concrete scream all the way across town. It was a freaking masterpiece. A giant fireball billowed into the sky, followed by spiraling black smoke. The fire threw off waves of heat and energy and I felt the life force leave the wood and bricks and metal girders as they melted and meshed into a new creation of my own making. The power they released washed over me like ocean breakers until my legs shook and my knees almost buckled and I spread my arms in pride and bliss.

Looking back, my happiest childhood moments were those times when I could pretend to sink my fingers into a blanket of thick rising smoke and let it lift me above the fire and carry me away on the wind. If that could only happen, all my shame and the petty little people in St. Bernard would be far below me. I'd look down on them and forget them the minute I looked away, onward and upward, and I'd never spend another minute in Dog Town.

I worked my way through an alternate high school for troubled kids, and then I wasted a year in college and studied welding in trade school. You know, the beauty of childhood crimes is that records are sealed. You can glide into adulthood with a spotless slate and nobody messes with you about any job you want. It was easier to cover up my past than to gloss over my poor eyesight, but with corrective lenses, I was physically qualified and I landed a job on the St. Bernard fire department.

Ironic, huh? Imagine me putting out fires.

I soon discovered that I simply wasn't suited for the down time involved in waiting for fires to happen. Boredom rattled me until I couldn't sit still, so I paced, talked non-stop, ate too much, and caused other firemen to leave the room. I tried to be a good co-worker, I really did. I studied training manuals for firemen and, under the heading of incendiary devices, I found something wonderful:

The least complicated detonation device is often the most effective.

It was the same point Dud had made, only he hadn't been as

concise, but then, he's Dud, right? For the first time in years, I reconsidered his concept of grenades made from simple things of nature and abundant materials at hand. I devoted months to tinkering with combustive formulas at work, tweaking chemistry until I realized where I'd gone wrong as a kid. I'd poured gasoline on the outside of potatoes when I should've put explosive chemicals *inside* them. After all, grenades had their explosives on the inside. Pull a pin, and this causes the chemicals to combine in the potent heart of the grenade, and boom! Potential is reached and destiny is fulfilled.

When my formula finally got close, I stole potatoes from the firehouse galley and injected them. I planned to take them to a clay pit and try them out that very afternoon, but unfortunately the day didn't go as I'd planned. Just at the end of my shift, our alarm went off and we had to jump into gear and head to a fire. In the confusion, I stored four potion-soaked potatoes in my locker.

We put out a fire in old man Wilson's recliner because he'd dozed off with a lit cigarette in the middle of *Final Jeopardy*. His La-Z-Boy was dripping in his front yard and we were winding up the hose when a dispatcher ordered us to hurry back to our station house. Rounding the last corner, we saw smoke boiling from the station's windows while a crowd gathered in the street. We had to endure the humiliation of putting out a fire at our own station in front of an audience of laughing spectators. Some of my co-workers thought our fire might've been caused by a lit cigarette left unattended in the rush, just like old man Wilson's recliner, but I knew better.

Before long, everybody knew.

To this day, I still can't say which potato reached critical mass in my closed locker. I thought the hard, raw potatoes I'd injected would be able to hold the chemicals in check, but the starch broke down too quickly. The volatile chemicals ran together inside the spuds, and that was that, technically speaking. The Louisiana state fire inspector who sniffed out the problem didn't care *how*, he only wanted to know *who*. He asked which fireman used that locker.

My lawyer told the courtroom that the fire was the result of an interrupted experiment to benefit mankind, but the stonewall southern judge couldn't relate. Students of history know the same thing happened to Oppenheimer after he invented the bombs. He looked into the atom and read the secrets of the universe, and it's understandable that people were cautious about a man with that much vision because he might look inside them, as well. When Oppenheimer said, "Now I am become Death, the destroyer of worlds," he was acknowledging everybody's fear of him. People acted as though there could be no safe place after that, and I suppose they were right, but not because of Oppenheimer. He never built another bomb.

By some miracle, I didn't do any jail time. The judge ruled that the station fire had been stupid, but accidental all the same. I was given probation and kicked off the job and labeled and laughed at, all because of an invention that did, in point of fact, work. I couldn't walk around town without somebody yelling "Hey, Tater!" at me, and what really pissed me off is that Dud shouted loudest. "Boy, you's a dumb kid and now you's a dumb man! Can't make no grenade outta no tater! I was only pullin your leg, didn't you know it?"

I hid at Mom's place for a few months until the ridicule quieted down, even though she teased me, like everybody else. She said, "Your father was touched in the head, Scout, and the potato doesn't fall far from the tree." Then she laughed like crazy. Don't worry, I was used to it, and I knew how to get around her. To feel better, I went out and lit up an abandoned house or two in a condemned neighborhood next to the airport. They were really gorgeous burns because there was a lot of oak in those houses. You may not be aware, but oak produces smoke that's almost pure white. I love the pearly smoke that billows out of oak like heavenly clouds. It holds together for a really long time before it finally spreads and floats just above the ground, fluffy and white as meringue on a pie.

Pine's different from oak. It generates dark, almost black, smoke caused by resin in the wood. Resin has a low ignition point. It's no trouble at all to light up pine, but I'm not a fan of black smoke, like it boiled out of hell's back door. I'd rather go to some trouble and get a smoke I can enjoy, like spruce and maple. Both have sugar in the wood and make yellowish, fragrant smoke that smells like scorched candy. I enjoy mahogany, too, because it's dense and burns blue-gray and billowy and leaves a heavy velvet haze.

The Vatican uses colored smoke when they elect a new pope. White smoke means they've made a decision, but black smoke means they can't agree. That smoke is a genuine religious experience because white is good and black is bad. It makes me wonder about the color of the smoke when people are cremated. Do people burn white like oak or black like pine? Maybe someday I'll find out.

WHEN I WAS staying at Mom's, there were times when I didn't feel like orchestrating a fire for weeks, so I pulled a hat over my face and spent time at the movies or down at the St. Bernard River where I've always found comfort. It's been more of a mother to me than my own mom, who invited me to move out of her house because she had a new boyfriend, and you won't believe who it was—my lawyer, no less. When I complained to her about it, she laughed at me and said, "Hey Scout, how do you like those appeals?" She got more action out of my court case then I did. Hope he's got a sense of humor. He'll need it.

So I was on the loose, on my own again, but I knew where to turn. I wanted to be close to my soothing river, so I applied for a small business loan and bought a fishing boat. Now I live on my loving, rocking river and earn a living supplying local restaurants with fish. That's why some people call me Trout Man, and that's okay, but memories are long in Dog Town and some people still call me Tater. Fortunately, I have all the fish I can eat, but I've developed a weird distaste for potatoes. Mom laughs and says I can't look one in the eye. She never changes.

Some nights, floating on the slow roll of the river, I'll catch the smell of smoke from a campfire and it sparks the arousal of a deep, persistent hunger. My stomach actually churns with longing, so I pull the boat ashore and go forth like a bridegroom to indulge my senses, to feel the warmth that touches and tightens my skin. I'll soon see the glorious release of energy in the form of heat and light, and smell sweet sap boiling in the cells of the wood as I watch smoke billow out in all colors of the rainbow. Oh my God, if I get close enough, I can see more rainbows dancing inside the flames and hear the crackling laughter of wood's metamorphosis, the most complete and satisfying transposition of matter that's possible on earth. It's mine alone, my creation, so exquisite. It speaks only to me. The fire builds until its power creates a mighty draft to fan the flames and I listen to the inferno's responsive roar as it rises and grows, its power made perfect by the grace of an elegant burn.

HUNGER: A LOVE STORY

"The dog's agenda is simple . . . I WANT."
~Caroline Knapp

DAYTIME, I'M FINE. Insulated. Distracted by routine. The bad times happen in my bunk at night. Bad times, for sure. That's when the memory monster steps out of my closet and stretches his warped old bones and grins at me. Then the vicious trickster proceeds to prolong and distort the night hours until they deepen into a twisted channel of recollection and sorrow. Remorse streams out of my head until I wonder if I'll simply drown in regret, one of these long nights.

Midnight introspection takes you round and round like a race track, but you never get anywhere because the end of one lap is the beginning of another, over the same old muddled ground. No matter how much bunk time analysis I've devoted to it, I still don't get closer to explaining the hunger, no more than I could describe the flow of blood through the heart. No logic, only the deep conviction that if I didn't have Wanda Mae Griggs for my own, my future was as final as the flat-line when a heart stops beating. Even at the end, when I was standing with all eyes on me, spending what might be the last few minutes of my life because of Wanda Mae, my brain was still buzzing her name.

I first saw her twelve years ago with the big-hair ladies. I was a scruffy bayou rat just turned eight, born in the dog days of August, when the blazing dog star Sirius lights up the eastern sky just before dawn, and the noon sun is hot enough to blow the lid off, like a pot boiling over. The excitement of my birthday was past, we were two weeks from a new school year, and my brother Johnny and I were low on entertaining prospects. We had no spending money, so town was out. We couldn't swim in Wolf Creek because the sun had lifted all the water out of the creek as surely as bread sops gravy. Stranded fish flopped and rotted on a ribbon of cracked mud. We gave in to death's fleeting diversion and kicked the stiffened fish around the creek bed and poked their glassy, dead eyes with sticks. I remember the awful stink they put off.

It's strange how the heart can recall a smell. Even after years, I recognize the tangible aromas of my childhood. I remember Mama's jelly cake, my brother's brassy sweat, and the clean soap smell of the big-hair ladies who drove into St. Bernard Parish every August in their Bible Bus, intent on giving us a holy ticket. They showed up to bestow the passport by which we could exist forever, in some cloud-filled place, in some form of vapor. Navigated by the Trinity, they rolled down the soft asphalt road to dip little country heathens in the icy fear of God.

Mama was leaving early for her job at the laundry when she said, "Big-hairs from Dog Town come this morning. You two go. You need somepin to do."

Johnny and I would just as soon skip it, but it got too hot to stay in our house once the August sun hit the low roof. All the dead fish had been poked eyeless, so we gave in and walked barefoot to the community center.

When we got near, Johnny pointed. "They here."

The Bible Bus sat crusted in road grit. We pushed inside the building where the big-hairs waited under the fans, sending out currents of clean smell, but we knew from past summers that by noon those stacks of hair would be wet strings stuck to their faces, and the flower skirts would be clinging to sweaty Christian legs.

A great deal of Southern anticipation has always focused on an afterlife, and the big-hairs were, in all aspects, a Southern phenomenon in touch with a golden hereafter. Their goal was to improve our lot once we came to eternal judgment; to make of us a valuable heavenly commodity, something worth keeping, least we be cast off the clouds to tumble down a reprobate's tunnel into a fiery hell. Their descriptions of damnation were specific and terrifying and made us desperate to become valuable in death. We absorbed Bible verses to quote for St. Peter at the Gates, and hymns to make Jesus clap along. They worked us up in sweat and fervor until we were the glass-eyed fish, gasping and near fainting from thirst.

At last, they handed out cookies, two apiece, and a few swallows of Kool Aid, lockjaw sweet, mixed in a dented aluminum soup pot with a single tray of ice. We were pitiful puppets eagerly lining up for the treats. One of the big-hairs ladled the lukewarm drink into white paper cones in our fists while another led us in song, swinging her arms like windshield wipers. We mumbled the hymns as we shuffled forward, cotton-mouthed and spellbound by the dripping ladle. When Johnny and I finally worked our way to the pot, the ladle lady looked us over, wondering if we were "brose," a regional term for brothers.

"You two ain't brose, are ya?" she asked, disbelieving.

It was a familiar question because we were so dissimilar. Johnny was blond, angelic, beautiful, especially when compared to my coarse homeliness. He was the image of Daddy, the handsome cad who'd left us. I looked like Mama; the reason he left.

I answered in a dry croak, "Yes ma'am, we brose."

The big hair eyed us while the suspended ladle dribbled my serving back into the pot. I couldn't keep my eyes off it. She persisted, "You got different daddies?"

Johnny shrugged but didn't answer. I said, "Same, far's we know. He left."

She nodded and emptied what little drink was left into my cup. I mumbled thanks and threw it down my throat and watched her pour Johnny's full share, but I didn't ask for more. I knew she'd only quote a Bible verse about gluttony.

She cooed at Johnny, "You're such a pretty little thang," as though it were his ticket out. "You could be in a movie. What's you boy's names?"

I put my hand out for my cookies and said, "Johnny White and Willie White."

Johnny batted long lashes and looked blandly past her. It was an early start. Over the years, he'd grow up with the ability to stare through women in that same way, rendering them stunned, defenseless, and eager. The big hair's attention bounced between us.

"Johnny and Willie? Which one's which?"

Before I could tell her, we were pushed down the line.

After refreshments, the big-hairs distributed tattered Bibles from a cardboard box. Thumbing the pages, I came across a crude graffiti revelation, my introduction to that special part of a girl, drawn like a flower on the index page by an earlier kid. I knew what it was, in the way boys know, and I realized I was seeing a thing God made, perfect, but forbidden all the same. In the middle of a prayer I elbowed Johnny and pointed, my finger just brushing the edge of it like I'd invented the thing. He glanced, casual as an archaeologist who's been shown a familiar specimen, and then he shrugged and tipped his head toward me. "That's a cooze," he whispered from the side of his mouth.

He was only a year older than me, but he knew—always knew—the dirty words, so many more than I did, and all the forbidden facts and flotsam. I was embarrassed by my innocence and I realized the drawing wasn't a discovery, wasn't a revelation, probably wasn't even accurate. It was simply a nasty picture, toilet stall art. I flipped the page so viciously it tore.

Wanda Mae was sitting in the row in front of us. She heard the page rip and glanced over her shoulder at me, looked down at the book and up again. I saw those blue eyes and that perfect mouth, and my heart jumped, never to beat normally again. She was a stranger to us all, old man Griggs's little golden granddaughter, recently sent to live with him. She looked me over, and Johnny next to me, and turned around in the dismissive way I would come to know so well.

"Uh, hey," I stammered at the back of her head. I immediately felt the punishing rap of a yardstick on my shoulder. The big hair didn't touch Wanda Mae, but I was happy to take the hit for her.

I tried to focus on the lesson about Creation, but the curve of Wanda Mae's ear was as pink and perfect as a clam shell and the skin on the back of her neck was smooth and tan. The big-hairs talked their way through Creation and got down to the business of human sin. They went on about Adam and Eve, the first two people on the rim of a sinless world. Soft, wispy curls stuck to Wanda Mae's sweaty neck and I could see a throb of pulse in her throat. Adam and Eve were punished for their lust. There was a tiny brown mole on the slope of her shoulder.

I should've paid attention to the big-hairs that day. Years later, Wanda Mae taught me a more explicit lesson in the power of lust to a degree that the big-hairs could hardly imagine. She showed me a hunger that I'd struggle to control all my life. From that stifling August day, she became my unattainable ideal, my dream girl, a blond, blue-eyed prize that Willie White would never possess, not in the longest hour of the best day of his life, but Johnny White could own any time he wanted.

I don't like to talk about it.

WHEN WE WERE kids, we had a yard dog named Brutus. He was a scruffy skinny flea bag, but stubborn, really stubborn. If Brutus closed his jaws around anything, you'd almost have to shoot him to make him let go. The dog was one of the few things my brother openly respected because Johnny and Brutus shared a kinship of pride and nobility that manifested as stubbornness and aggression. Even after Brutus was dead and buried, Johnny kept the name. He's on the bare knuckle boxing circuit now, fighting under the moniker "Brutus the Brute."

Bare knuckle's not strictly legal, but lawmen look the other way because it's highly lucrative if you're a gambling man, so they shed their uniforms and come to the fights to place their bets, just like everybody else. Most of the time, they put their money on Brutus the Brute, because cops are trained to recognize the type of stubborn guy who can't let go and won't back down until somebody shoots him. I can't imagine what goes on in a man's head that would make him step into a roped-off square and let another man beat him senseless. Who would volunteer for it, as a profession? But there's a lot about Johnny that mystifies me; the man he became, and how others regard him. He's never really lived in the world with the rest of us; he just looks down on us from whatever lofty place he occupies. Nothing affects him, but he still draws people like iron filings to a magnet, and they flock to watch him fight.

Every few weeks, Johnny comes home to see Mama and me and he gives us some of the money he's earned from the fights. On the road, he bets on himself to win, so he has the double motivations of pride and profit. There are always new scars and healing cuts sewn with thread; crusty lines like a road map of all the places he's been and fists he's stopped with his jaw or the circle of bone around his eyes.

I was on the bottom bunk with a magazine and I watched him peel off his shirt. I'm skinny like Mama, just an awkward bundle of sticks tied together, but Johnny's everything I'm not, with his long, smooth mounds of muscle. Even the scars don't make him ugly; they make him thrilling. I saw bruises on his ribs, big purple and yellow stains, and I asked him if they hurt.

"Not right off. Pain don't come till later."

"You're full of scars," I said.

He answered, "Take fire into ya bosom, ya get burned."

I put down my magazine. "What fire?"

He folded his shirt and laid it on a chair. "It's in the Bible."

"They had bare knuckle back then?"

"Jesus Christ, Willie, you're such a dumb shit."

"Not dumb, I'm in community college now. You oughta know, you pay for it."

"Yeah, all the good it does me. I still bunk with a stupid shit."

"At least nobody pounds me, like you get pounded."

"You're pounded too, little brother, just a different way. Everybody's pounded, trust me on that."

He put on his great blank face and jumped on the upper bunk graceful as a cat. Bedsprings squeaked under the weight of his perfection. I knew he didn't believe I was stupid, but a tough guy can't step out of the role, and he can't stop getting pounded and bringing home the blood money. That was his brutal reality, and the only type of formal education he'd ever get.

I had other identities too: college boy, part-time car detailer at the Super Lube, wiper of windshield bugs, plucker of used condoms, those little latex snake skins stuck to the floorboards, and, most important of all, I was the future husband of Wanda Mae Griggs, at least in my dreams. I had a long way to go before that last one came true. Even after the accident, when she was on crutches, Wanda Mae was still really stuck-up for a one-legged girl. I was dirt under her only remaining foot.

I had just one night with her, before she lost her leg, when she asked me to take her to the Lube after closing to ride the hydraulic lift because she was fascinated by machinery. When we got there, moonlight was shining through into the service bay and there was a familiar smell of exhaust fumes, like the ghosts of highway dreams. I drove onto the lift and up we went. She was grinning and her eyes had a radioactive shine. Her skin was perfect and her blond hair glowed in the moonlight. After all my waiting and all my dreams, I finally got lucky with her that night, on the car seat, up on that lift. For a few minutes, I thought I owned her. I believed she wanted to be owned, and maybe she did, for about five minutes. But when the lift came down, she asked me to call Johnny so we could all go get a drink. I just took her home because it hurt to look at her, and I went out and got drunk alone and cried in my beer like a baby because Wanda Mae didn't love me yet.

The next day I called her and left a message. I waited for days, but she didn't call me back, and after a while, what happened on the lift wasn't real any more. It should've been the most earth-shaking thing that ever was, but I started forgetting the details and getting them confused with my daydreams until I wasn't sure what was real. I had fantasized about her so often that truth blended with imagination and it all spun into just another hollow dream of Wanda Mae.

A FEW WEEKS after that night at the Lube, Wanda Mae picked out her next fool.

Billy Green's daddy was a rich farmer, so she asked Billy for a ride on the farm's big thrasher. He agreed, and it was the worst mistake of his life, and hers too, but out of everybody in town, I most clearly understood how persuasive Wanda Mae could be when she wanted something. From the minute she asked him, Billy was a goner, a sucker, and a victim. He was a three-course meal.

The way Billy tells it, he and Wanda Mae were on the driver's seat of the thrasher, steering it through a field. She could feel the rumble of the engine through the seat, but she said it wasn't intense enough, so she crawled on the hood where the vibrations were stronger. She was laughing, Billy said, even when he shouted for her to come back. She turned her head to laugh at him, to tell him she could do as she pleased, and that's when she lost her balance. She slid forward and her left leg plunged into the spinning blades.

Round and round went the blades, slicing, slicing, while she screamed for Billy or God or somebody. Billy could've simply turned the key and killed the motor, but in his panic, he never thought of it. He said he was screaming too, as he scurried onto the hood and went sliding in her blood. He made a blind grab for her flailing arms and pulled with all his might while her blood sprayed in his eyes and hair and soaked his shirt. By the time he pulled her free, she'd stopped screaming. He yelled her name and shook her and she flopped like a blood soaked rag, so he thought she must be dead. How could she live, after all the screaming and so much spilled blood? But it turned out she wasn't dead, just close to it. He gathered her limp body in his arms and ran to his truck and got her to the hospital just before she completely bled out on his upholstery.

She was still connected to the shredded leg, barely, but it was filleted to the bone, so they couldn't save it. To Wanda Mae's way of thinking, the necessity for amputation magically became Billy's fault. After the surgery, she had only contempt for Billy and she refused to see him, even though he sat for hours in the hall outside her room with a bouquet of wilting flowers in his hand.

Sure as hornets are drawn to sugar, a swarm of lawyers buzzed around her bed and assured her that Billy's insurance money would make everything all right. Wanda Mae's body parts were shrewdly estimated in dollars so that lawsuits could be filed. Eventually, she left the hospital and hobbled around town on crutches while the toxic landslide of barristers amassed a mountain of claims and the haggling dragged on. She became a regular sight on the streets and I remember the day she called to me while I was walking to lunch.

"Willie! Wait up!" she shouted.

The modified, now one-legged Wanda Mae hurried toward me, swinging between the crutches, her gripping hands white-knuckled on the crossbars. My heart flopped with excitement and embarrassment for her when one of the crutches went into a pothole and she stumbled, so I acted like I didn't see. She finally reached me, breathing hard.

"Hi," she said, and smiled her perfect smile.

Her face was stunning and the sky exploded inside my head because most of her, the best parts anyway, remained intact to an extent that still enchanted me. Her bizarre tragedy made her exotic, and all that dramatic suffering gave her regality. Her greeting of "Hi" spun out of her mouth in slow motion, sliding between her lips like a curling ribbon in the air. I saw sunlight on her golden hair and I remembered moonlight at the Lube and the pressure of her warm legs wrapped around me on the lift, and my mouth went dry.

Every indication led me to believe that she was going to say something I'd waited so long to hear. She was going to ask me how I'd been, and did I want to get a beer. She'd say that she missed me and maybe we should spend the night together, a graceful perfumed proposition. I suppressed the urge to say yes, yes, before the offer was even formed. I watched her draw a breath, I waited, and then she said the words, only three words, in the form of a question.

Is Johnny home?

A sudden grind of gears in my brain made me dizzy. I think I even staggered. She might as well have broadsided me with a crutch, because her question knocked the breath out of me. I could barely inhale, but somehow I managed to say Johnny was still on the road and her eyes slid off me like I wasn't worth seeing. Think about looking through a window and not seeing the pane of glass, only what's beyond. That's what it was like. The sun dropped heavy heat and eighteen-wheelers roared on the highway, throwing sheets of exhaust. Somebody was frying onions in the diner. Music blared from a cruising car and I could smell the dust its tires lifted off the blacktop. All the details of the day were there, except for me. I was a pane of glass. Somewhere below it all, in the basement of whatever manhood I still possessed, I wondered what it would be like to hurt her, really hurt her, a crippled girl, on purpose.

She mumbled a disappointed goodbye and moved away, three-pointed crutch walking, each gesture slow and full of purpose, and I conjured the image of a giant praying mantis that bites off the head of her mate, once she's done with him.

A FEW MONTHS later, Wanda Mae's case settled. She used the money to buy a titanium leg. This led to lurid contemplation by the Super Lube guys, who speculated how it would feel with her on bottom, her real leg in the air on one side and titanium on the other, waving like an antenna that could pick up Houston if she held it in the right direction. Johnny could've told them what it was like: *That's a cooze.*

After Wanda Mae's case settled, people began casting around for a new diversion, and we got it when the snake show came to St. Bernard. After that, everybody talked about me instead of Wanda Mae, because the show ended my life as I'd known it and marked the death all my grand plans and dreams and any future I ever hoped to have.

The snake people set up a tent on the vacant lot where the Western Auto burned down. I'm talking about a traveling spectacle under patched canvas, run by a pale man with flashy jewelry, slick hair, and a talent for handling poisonous reptiles. He brought snakes in cracked aquariums, plus a couple of lizards from south of the border. He had a musical band called The Burning Sensations, and there was a girl singer in a low-cut dress.

I didn't want to go, but Johnny was home and he was keen to see the show. He'd heard about the singer's big tits, not store-bought, he said, those pups were real, two giant yeast rolls bubbling out of the top of her dress. He scraped together ticket money for both of us, real fast.

When we got to the tent, silent heat lightning flashed like white neon behind the clouds. The night air smelled of ozone. There was a soft, distant roll of thunder, and the wind was making the sides of the tent whip and belly. At the entrance, an old man took our money and counted change with scaly hands and thick yellow fingernails. The smell of him was like somebody pissed in a glass of sour milk.

Johnny paid our admission and we stepped through the flap and sat on folding chairs. Soon we were sweating in the trapped heat. The air was thick with the funk of feet and manure on boots and Dollar General perfume and the raw smell of the pine lumber they'd used to build the stage. There was another odor too, of cold-blooded creatures that were never meant to be in aquariums, the dark, organic stink of an old grave or a snake's nest. I thought of flipping over a rock where crawling things squirm from the light. The air was glassy with the glare of bare light bulbs overhead, swinging in the wind every time the tent flap opened.

Suddenly my stomach grabbed because I spotted Wanda Mae on the front row with her new titanium leg. One of her friends whispered to her and she turned and scanned the crowd over her shoulder until her eyes found Johnny. What a ripping, raw look she gave him, starving, like a lost dog desperately begging from person to person in a parking lot.

Johnny saw the way she looked at him and he said to me, "Been there, done that."

The heat, the smells, the sight of Wanda Mae, Johnny's attitude, all combined to make me feel like I might throw up, but Johnny simply put on his great blank face and stared ahead like Wanda Mae was just another smell in the air. She whipped her head around to the front so fast it must've hurt her neck.

That's when the snake man stepped from behind a curtain to scattered applause and distracted me. I tried to concentrate on the show. He introduced his band and gave them a count (one-ana, two-ana). The Burning Sensations broke into a version of "Love Me Tender" while he introduced the "Lovely Lady of Song." Her name was—I'll never forget it—LaVetta, and the rumors about her tits were right on target. She sang and jiggled and breathed the stagnant air. Every time she took a gasp, her dress stretched tighter. The guys in the audience gasped along with her until LaVetta had every man in the tent light-headed on oxygen.

Johnny said, "I might ask her for a date later."

"Yeah, sure, go for it," I said.

"You think I can't get some of that?"

I shrugged. "Anybody in this tent can get some of that, for a price. It's like the Hokey Pokey, dude. That's what it's all about."

The snake fellow strutted forward and looked down at the hicks in the tent. He said a few words about poisonous reptiles from Egypt and the wilds of Borneo and held up a snake in a cage. He informed us it was from India, which he pronounced "In-Jah." Johnny raised his hand and asked what kind of snake it was. The man thought for a minute and said, "It's a Gunga-Din."

Johnny leaned over to me and whispered, "I heard o' that."

The snake man described Cleopatra's death by snake bite while LaVetta demonstrated by putting a poisonous asp to her breast and falling dead. Her dress rode up when she fell, and we all jumped to our feet. She earned a round of applause that got more enthusiastic when she took a deep bow.

They dropped the lights and played eerie flute music while the snake man pulled snakes out and flipped them, doing his stunts. I saw sweat pop out on Wanda Mae's neck until she glowed like a watch dial. She just couldn't get enough of a man flirting with death. I was jealous over the way she looked at Johnny and how much she admired the snake man, and that must've accounted for what I did next, because it wasn't well thought out. When the snake man called for a volunteer from the audience, I jumped to my feet. Johnny made a grab to hold me back, but he came up empty. I ran down the aisle and hopped on stage.

"You surely are eager to look death in the eye," the snake man said.

He smelled like hair oil and cigs and he was wearing women's makeup smeared with sweat. The first drops of rain thumped on the roof of the tent, but I didn't think about it because I looked down at Wanda Mae on the front row. I was hoping I'd look good to her up on stage. I didn't plan on looking like a damn fool. I accomplished that without any plan at all.

"I'm going to hypnotize this deadly viper," said the snake man. He waved a poisonous water moccasin in my face. We'd seen them in Wolf Creek, "mocs" we called them; fanged death hiding in the murky current like a spirit in the water, stealing lives with a single bite. The snake man held the moccasin's head between his thumb and forefinger and it flicked its pink tongue at me.

He said, "I'm going to drape this lethal snake over your neck, young man." (There was a gasp from the crowd.) "Don't worry folks, no harm will come to this young fellow if he stays perfectly still." He said it loud, to be heard over the pounding rain. "Are you ready to start?" he asked me.

My scalp crawled as if one of his lizards had skittered across it. "Okay," I said through my teeth. I was wishing I'd worn nicer clothes. I still had on my Lube shirt with *Willie* sewn on the pocket, like the label on a can of potted meat. The snake man glanced at my name. "Can you keep perfectly still, Willie?"

I gave the snake man a nod. He began to hypnotize the snake, although he was actually pinching off its air. The moc suddenly went limp as rope, mouth open and tongue hanging out. The snake man looped the moc around my neck like a lover draping a diamond necklace over a woman's throat. I felt the weight and the cool brown scales against the back of my neck. I was hoping Wanda Mae didn't know how terrified I was. But no, she was watching me with sparkling eyes and I wasn't transparent any more.

What the snake could do to me didn't matter, because Wanda Mae was looking at me in the same radioactive way she looked at Johnny. I'd wanted her for her for so long, like Adam had waited, restless and unsatisfied, hungry for something he couldn't name. I pictured Adam's excitement, the slick thrill of his nakedness, focusing on the glow in Eve's eyes when she handed the apple to him with a hunk missing, the juice still on her chin. Adam in the coolness of the shade, the taste of apple in his teeth. I pictured the snake strutting on its scaly legs before God thrashed them off. The snake was leaning on Adam's shoulder, explaining about Eve, whispering in Adam's ear: *That's a cooze . . .*

I couldn't play it cool any more. I would've burned in hell to have Wanda Mae, and that tent was hell for all I knew; it was hot enough. The rain was pounding, pounding, and my head was dull, not the same as being drunk or high, but sluggish, like waking from deep sleep. I was twitching, sparks were pinging inside me, and heat spread into my hands and shot off my fingertips like ten clean spark plugs. Fire inside and heat outside; I was burning up. Sweat ran into my eyes and made Wanda Mae only a blur.

I forgot the snake man's warning to be still. I raised my right hand, a hand full of heat and spark, to wipe my eyes so I could see Wanda

Mae's perfect face. As I reached up, I heard a sound, somewhere past the heat and the noise of the rain, beyond my vision of Adam's cool green garden. I heard Johnny's voice, far away and desperate, scream WILLIE! NO-O-O!

MAMA SAYS THE human soul is a cup of sadness. When you cry enough tears to fill the cup, you die. Happiness doesn't fulfill your soul; only grief can do that. I've cried plenty of times over the years, but not enough, because I didn't die on that stage. Johnny ran forward while the fangs were still in my hand and pulled the snake off and flung it. He whipped his belt around my wrist like a tourniquet and lifted me in his arms. Everybody was running and knocking over chairs. In the confusion, the snake man and his bunch made a well-greased escape and vanished into the rain. Their abandoned tent flapped in the wind for a few weeks until the sheriff finally hauled it away.

I was in the hospital for twenty days and I've been home two months. I can't remember the first couple of days after the bite. The details burned away inside the fever from the poison and infection, so Johnny was right; when you're in that kind of heat, the pain doesn't come until later. My hand turned black and swelled big as a football and the skin split like Adam's rotten fruit. My fingernails peeled away and a smell like dead fish drifted up. The doctor tried to save my hand, but after a few days, he cut it off a little above the wrist.

The doctor said I'm lucky because Johnny's belt stopped the venom from spreading through my body, but I don't feel lucky. Not at all. I think I feel the poison still inside me, dark oily globs like the mud at the bottom of the river, sliding through my veins, riding the waves of my blood, settling like sludge. I sense it, like I sense when a stranger is staring at the empty end of my sleeve.

A scream bounces in my head and slams against my skull. Mama says the scream is the sound of my hollow soul, a cup of sadness slowing filling up. The hospital shrink said it's an inner scream of grief and loss. He handed me my discharge papers and told me to go and live my life, but it's not that simple.

Wanda Mae and I both lost a part of our bodies to foolishness, but she didn't call me and never came to see me in the hospital. There was a time when I believed we'd shared a moment in the tent, but now I know she was glowing because Johnny was near. I was a means to an end, a pane of glass that didn't count. Yeah, been there, done that.

I'm a freak, and everybody's talking about me and about what happened to me, and how stupid it was, so I hide in the house. I've lost the ordinary things: thunderstorms, roads baking in the heat, fields of cows, dance hall music, bar fights and hardware stores, groups of pretty girls on street corners, rubbing soap on a washcloth, drying off with a towel, shifting gears in my car, going to class and taking notes, frying an egg, cutting a steak, zipping my pants. I never knew so many things were two-handed.

Johnny says to take the first step. He says the first punch always hurts the worst, but everything after that is just another blow. My first step is to learn to operate this hook so I can get back to work and back to school. For now, I've got some bitching pain medicine, all I want, day and night. Barbiturates. Johnny calls them "barbies."

I stay inside and take my barbies and listen to the noise of the world through the windows. Out there, everything moves in slow motion. Cars on the road pass with the crawl of a funeral. Afternoon rain comes down without a sound. I'm riding a gradual slide of time. I sleep a lot, thanks to the barbies, and sometimes I dream of running and diving into water that tumbles and bubbles and sounds like pretty girls laughing.

Mama talks, Johnny talks, and their mouths send waves of sound that float and curl around the half-eaten bags of chips on the coffee table and slide down the curtains and weave through the twisted sheets on my bed. Mama says life is in the details that stack up and fill our emptiness like pennies fill a jar. I don't know details. I only know that there's light, and there's dark. I prefer the dark.

At night when I'm alone in my bunk, I have the lub-dub of my heartbeat in my ears. I hear the pop and hum of the fridge, and the soft crunch of Johnny's shoes when he sneaks in late, smelling of sweat and hormones and some girl's perfume. There's a round white moon outside my window and a round rust spot on the sink where the faucet drips with a silly gurgle, each clear drop forming a perfect pearl of falling water until it hits and disappears.

Every world, even a dark world, is filled with details.

BEAR, PART ONE:
MONGRELS AND MONSTERS

"Of course when you were running with the bottom dogs, what you mostly saw were paws, claws, and assholes."
~Stephen King: *Doctor Sleep*

OUR WATER WORLD was apart, but not isolated. We had accessible portals to realms far beyond our secluded swampland. Shallow coves and bays flowed serenely into larger, cooler bodies of navigable water. Peninsulas connected to hospitable terrain supporting cities so vast that their shiny complexity would've astounded us, had we ever seen them. Greyhound buses and Japanese cars rolled smoothly on delta roads and Louisiana highways. We even had an airport in the nearby town of St. Bernard. Not a thing held us in our boondocks bayou except our own arrogance, our justifiable fear of the unknown, and withering poverty. We stayed in and kept the rest out. We might as well have lived on an island slowly circled by sea monsters.

It was in this sphere of exclusion that I crossed fate with Charlie LaForce some twenty years ago, when we were sapling boys, all elbows and angles, with the sudden long bones of puberty. We were two ornery sons of poverty in a delta ravaged by an August drought. The swamp was drying up, our childhood was winding down, and we didn't mean a thing to a soul from outside, except for the fact that we'd reached an age to be put on the list.

I recognized trouble the minute I saw it driving up the road that morning. They had the list in hand, that bunch of butchers, and here they come in their white government van that welled up like a pale ghost in the mist. They threw a rooster tail of dirt off the tires and left a dust cloud. Only feds and outlaws tore it up like that on the clay.

Bayou people peeked from behind curtains or scrutinized from porch sofas as the big white box sped past. Papa and I peered down from our roof where we were hammering shingles. In his distraction, Papa hammered his thumb and a string of Cajun curses cut into a morning that had suddenly turned impending. The whole bayou dropped into watchful quiet, broken by the growl of their engine and screech of springs bouncing on the washboard road.

The van rolled up to the community health clinic in a dust billow. Two county nurses climbed out, honking and snapping like big gray geese, and they disappeared into the peeling concrete building where we routinely got shots and check-ups and a handful of any pills we wanted, if the doctor was drunk enough.

Those nurses had an objectionable job ahead, so they quickly set up shop, assisted by the same two deputies who usually busted us for underage drinking, underage around here meaning fourteen or fifteen. We knew these deputies well; I should say we knew them intimately. Both of them took a fancy to pulling us over in our shitty, oil-burning heaps so that they could molest us in the guise of a shakedown. Whichever one stopped us, they were equally bad. We had to deal with not one monster, but two.

To this day, I can't tell you why a man becomes a monster. I suppose certain men are born to it, but monsters can't be predicted or explained. They are what they are, a force of nature, all action and no consequence, free of the burden of conscience. Monsters have an inner pressure to release, a trajectory to follow, so they act, in the same way that volcanoes erupt or giant meteors collide with earth. We simply get in their way or cross paths with them at the wrong time and they mow us down. If you live long enough in this world, they'll find you. It's what they do.

The deputy we called "Tom Thumb" had a taste for boys. He'd order us out of the car, then he'd pat us down for drugs, sliding his hand up the inseam of our pants, cupping our crotches, and squeezing viciously with his thumb on a testicle. The pain was akin to a tenpenny nail driven clear through, front to back. We'd gasp and grimace and lean on the side of the car, fighting a surge of nausea while he strutted and smiled. We knew it was more about power than contraband or even sex, but the pain and revulsion were real, all the same. There was no way to brace for it, so we just took it.

The other monster, "Lester Molester," liked to search our girlfriends for drugs, especially in her bra, if she wore one, or he'd make her get out of the car and order her to put her hands on the front fender to give her boyfriend a helpless view through the windshield. He'd come up from behind and kick her feet apart and take it from there. "You dig that?" he'd ask, his hands busy in her pants. He'd press himself against her back. "You little bitch, you like this, don't you?"

She'd be sobbing by the time Lester was finished, so there was nothing to do but drive her home. Lester knew she'd never tell her folks what he'd done because she was standard white trash, meaning her daddy operated a still, or poached, or ran stolen guns, or found a stretch of swamp ground not shaded by cypress trees where he could seed a crop of damn fine weed in the loamy soil. He watched over his plants more tenderly than he did his own children. Anonymity was crucial for keeping various family enterprises going and not busted by the law. All those secrets were food on the table, so when his little girl finally broke down and told him, big daddy would feel bad, but he'd let it go because he had a family to feed and a business to run. Most important, he had a lawman in his pocket, one with an understanding of kick-back, and this arrangement was valued and nurtured, even if a pretty daughter was a commodity in the deal.

I didn't tell my father, either, to keep him from making a fuss. He was a kind man who pumped unspeakable muck out of septic tanks for a living and I didn't want him to end up at the bottom of one of the tanks. A fuss would be inconvenient for the law, but downright destructive for community enterprises. A hammer to the back of the head could come from any direction.

We recognized those two nurses, too. They showed up at the clinic from time to time to put us through one thing or another, for public health, or so they said. We knew this visit was on orders from some petty government tool justifying his paycheck. The nurses were, in general, a bitter and indifferent pair. I won't say they were brutal, necessarily, but they saw us as less than human, and that made them more hazardous than the deputies, because they had access to drugs and medical instruments and plenty of leeway, but no supervision, oversight, or accountability.

That day, they showed up with a list of bayou bad boys, known local teenage thugs. The visitors intended to assert authority over young punks on the list; polecats the law would have to deal with in full force before long, once we grew into our criminal destiny. Given time, a molested scrotum wouldn't keep us in line. We'd refine our larceny to the point that underage drinking was the least of the troubles we caused. Discord was a bayou tradition, our birthright, and there wasn't a delta family that didn't have an uncle, brother, son, or daddy pressing out license plates in the state pen or hoeing rows at the prison farm.

Tom Thumb and Lester Molester took the list of names and went on a mongrel hunt, door to door, fish camp to fish camp. By late morning they had us, at least most of us, herded into the clinic where the nurses popped on rubber gloves. That scared me. I wasn't one for tissue samples and needles, but this time they only probed our heads for lice. The few who showed no symptoms were sprayed with poison for the hell of it, frisked for good measure, and sent out the door with empty pockets. They left behind a stockpile of pocket knives and skinning blades, beer openers and fishing gaffs. The swamp's a dangerous place if you're unarmed. Wasn't a bayou boy that didn't carry a sharp.

The rest of us mongrels, the vermin-infested lads, were stripped of shirts and shoes. This stripping was a lesson, to let us know we had no place to hide. We clustered, awkward and embarrassed, the bones of our bodies rising narrow and angular, like the skeletal framework of tall buildings under construction; that type of skyscrapers few of us would ever see for real.

By this time of day the clinic was an oven, no air conditioning for the likes of us, and we were shining with sweat. We lined up for frisking by Lester's professional fingers, lost our knives and protection tools. When he finished, he took up the list and began calling role. After a few names, I heard, "Bear Lonnier!"

I raised my hand. "Here."

A rough grip circled my upper arm, a rude tug. Tom Thumb

shoved me into the raggedy line.

"Charlie LaForce!"

"Yo!"

Charlie was jammed in line behind me. I'd seen him around, but we weren't friends. He was a non-student, a truant who didn't come to school all that much, but nobody cared because he was a "Deep-in" from a community of misfits who lived deep in the swamp in a closed, floating colony of houseboats off the grid, no electricity or roads, only kinfolk, dogs, and secrets. The Deep-ins didn't have addresses; they didn't get mail. They didn't pay taxes or obey ordinances or abide strangers. They were generally crooks and criminals, trappers and runners and thieves, only a step above the creatures they caught and ate. They spoke a form of Cajun all their own, and when their younguns bothered to show up at school, usually in pairs, we snubbed and feared them. They were ghosts in the halls because there's no place on earth where a pecking order's more defined than the cruel corridors of high school. It was sheer bad luck that put Charlie in the grip of deputies that day. He'd been sent into town for supplies and they simply nabbed him. Wrong place, bad time, mowed down. He was the only Deep-in boy they netted, and later, when he showed up at home with his head shaved, he'd probably take a beating for attracting the attention of the law.

By the time Lester finished calling role, a long undulating line of lice boys snaked through the clinic. Lester was posted back of the line. He barked at us to keep our eyes front, no sneaking away, no talking in line. Shirtless and shoeless, deprived of weaponry, our heads crawling with vermin, we worked our way in barefoot disgrace toward a cutting chair.

A whisper passed down the line . . . those two butcher nurses up ahead were using sheep shears on us. Sheep shears for chrissake; intended for clipping animals. Up front, Tom Thumb walked a path around the cutting chair, round and round through a growing carpet of hair. We itched and scratched and trickled sweat as we watched boys in front take the gray metal chair fully haired and rise shorn to the raw scalp and gagging in a cloud of louse spray. Tom Thumb circled the chair like a shark, the leather of his gun belt creaking, his polished shoes muffled by a pad of hair on the floor. We dipped our heads and shuffled wordlessly in time to the monotonous buzz of shears, slowly gaining on the same fate as those who'd gone before. Eyes front. No talking, no sneaking.

Finally, my turn came. Just before they led me to the chair, I felt three gentle raps of fingertips between my bare shoulder blades.

Tap, tap, tap.

This, as it turned out, was my intimate introduction to Charlie LaForce. I glanced back and he quickly looked down and studied his bare feet as though he hadn't done it. I had the grounded, earthy build of a boxer and I enjoyed a good brawl, everybody knew it, but I decided to give his taps a pass. In my arrogance, I reckoned I'd been touched out of admiration, as a gesture of respect by a lesser boy, a Deep-in from a stagnant green water world. I shrugged him off and turned to face the cutting chair.

Behind me, Charlie leaned in and whispered, "Dat's fo' luck, Bear."

His use of my name, the unwelcome familiarity, shocked me, but before I could respond, Tom Thumb poked me in the side with a billy club. "Sit!" he ordered.

The two nurses stood on either side of the looming chair. One of them held clippers, the other juggled a big, awkward pump sprayer, the kind exterminators use. I took a seat, dropped my chin to my chest, and bore my rough turn under the buzzer, grimacing at the yanking and jerking. My neck muscles ached from resisting, and tears stung my eyes. I thought of Tom's thumb on my scrotum, Lester's rough hands on my girlfriend. (You dig that?) Long wisps of cut hair brushed down my shoulders and chest and stuck to my sweaty back. I picked up a strand from my lap and studied it. I didn't see bugs in it. It was just my hair, dark and silky, my best feature. The rest of me was coarse and unremarkable, like my namesake, the swamp bear.

The hum stopped and I sighed and relaxed, thankful my shaming was over, but it wasn't, as I found out. The clipping nurse began her spiel, "All right, now hold your breath, close your . . ."

Without warning, a sudden, choking cloud of poison was pumped onto my head. The clipping nurse yelled, "Dammit, how many times do I have to tell you? Wait til I tell em to hold their breath!"

"Sorry," mumbled the pumper, and hung her head. She apologized to the clipper nurse, but she'd done it to me.

The sprayed poison was an instant cap of fire, stinging hundreds of raw abrasions. I gasped with pain and shock and my sudden intake of breath pulled strangling insecticide into my lungs. Toxins coated my throat and I exploded in violent coughing. Tom Thumb barked at me to get out of the chair. When I didn't immediately respond, he came from behind and slid his fingers into my armpits. With a grunt, he hoisted me onto my feet and gave me a brutal push. I stumbled forward and barely kept my footing in the slippery tangle of hair as I made a blind rush for the exit and fresh air.

Outside, the sudden glare of sunlight disoriented me even more. I bent forward with my hands on my knees for balance, gasped and panted, coughed, gagged, and vomited against the building. When it was all out, I swiped at tears running down my cheeks, flung snot off my upper lip, hacked and spat until I was dry, then I lurched toward the outside faucet.

A few boys had already gathered there, taking turns at the water, running the flow through their mouths and out again. They cupped their hands under the stream and dumped water on their raw scalps. They waved me ahead and I dropped to my knees and opened my mouth under the stream. The water was warm and metallic, channeled through iron pipes. My stomach gurgled and cramped around airy gulps, but I kept it down. Somebody extended a hand and pulled me to my feet. I threw my head back and spit the last mouthful in an arc that sparkled in the sun.

I walked to the building, leaned my back against the wall, and took shallow breaths to control the cough. The sky was cloudless and the sun threw welcome heat on my ravaged scalp. I was grateful that the wall was warm and solid, a comfort. A poisonous stink coated my sinuses and bitterness dripped down my throat. My ears rang. I trembled and twitched from adrenaline. We were all twitching, flexing our shoulders, belching tap water and clearing our throats like a chorus of frogs. There were no monster deputies out here. We were free of their clicking shoes and creaking holsters; the repetitious dry thump of billy club against cupped hand, their brutal agendas and trajectories.

Some boys were waiting for friends or brothers still inside, so we hung around killing time, a cluster of hairless monks, pacing, dripping, swinging our arms like huffing bully boys. I saw half of the Foley twins, don't know if he was Leroy or Leon, I never could tell them apart. There was Tony LeCaste and his cousin Bo, both classmates of mine. Hector Mull and his half-brother Skeeter were at the water faucet. There were others I didn't recognize because they'd dropped out of school early to fish and hunt with their fathers and put meat on the table. Formal education wasn't much good unless you had hopes of breaking away from the bayou for the wider world, but escape didn't happen all that much. A boy's father showed him what he needed to know to survive four-legged brutes of the swampland. We learned to get the better of merciless nature and hungry wildlife. If a guy didn't have a father, he joined the army and a drill sergeant took over his training. Uncle Sam taught him how to carry a rifle in a foreign land where his opponents had two legs instead of four. Otherwise, the survival lessons weren't all that different: head down, eyes open, don't get eaten.

The Foley twin, Leroy or Leon, told me that Blaise Antoine and his cousin Nick had run out the door like bulls through a chute and disappeared into the trees without pausing to speak or drink, without even their pocket knives to keep the swamp at bay. They'd rather take their chances in the brackish water and cypress trees. We knew those boys were clever, though, and good hunters. They'd show up in a couple of days, still shirtless and shoeless, with stubble scalps, fresh hides, and skinning tools crafted from the sharp, pearly edges of oyster shells.

I heard buzzing through the open door and knew the nurses were shearing the fragile Deep-in kid in line behind me. Before long, the noise abruptly stopped, replaced by violent coughing. The gagging and hacking moved closer to the door and suddenly Charlie stumbled out, stinking, gasping, glazed by shock, squinting in the glare, lurching on his long legs. I was older but Charlie was taller, lanky and frail, with an arched bony spine.

I saw what they'd done to him, to all of us. We'd endured the shearing so passively, without a word of protest, because it was our fate, just as we endured Tom's thumb and Lester's fingers. My grandpa told me that fate's a coin, good on one side, bad on the other, but I didn't see fate as having two sides. To me, fate was four walls, a cage, a man-made box that none of us could escape.

It had been a long, brutalizing day and we all needed a laugh, if any bunch ever did. I decided to have a go at Charlie for the benefit of my friends hanging around, to scare him and watch him take off like a whipped dog. I'd hack at him the way Tom and Lester hacked at us. Luck was a pecking order, that's all, just a pecking order. You passed bad luck along. We needed a boost to get back on top and the other boys needed a hero, a champion. Charlie was nothing to me, so I'd stand on him to make myself a little taller.

I yelled, "Hey you! Deep-in!"

The guys knew me and knew what was coming, so they grinned and pulled together to watch me deal it out to a Deep-in kid. At that minute, the little Cajun boy didn't have a friend in the whole bunch of us. Charlie heard me and stopped with his shirtless back to me. I ran up with a war whoop, pulled back my fist, and watched him brace to be hit from behind. I thought he'd run, I hadn't figured he'd hold his ground and take the blow. I could make out the curve of ribs through his skin, the knobs of spine and the insubstantial plates of his shoulder blades. He was nothing but a walking backbone covered in bruises, some fading, some new. It was a familiar story, not enough at home to eat but plenty of abuse, served up regularly. The nurses had seen his bare back, they must've noticed his thinness and bruises, but nobody bothered to ask, nobody cared to intervene.

Charlie wouldn't run away on those stick legs, but he wouldn't fight me either, so I had a problem. I wanted to scare him, not hit him, especially since I'd seen him up close, but I couldn't quit; I had to do something to him for the sake of my audience. I thought of agendas and trajectories, of consequences, of crossing paths, and how often I'd paid that price myself. I stopped short, and instead of taking a swing, I reached up and ran my hand over his head, repeating what he'd said to me, "That's for luck." There was an organic, bony roundness to his skull and a prickly crawl as I slid my palm over his scalp. Behind me, the boys were laughing at what they thought was a planned joke.

I said, "Gotcha, Deep-in. Did I scare ya?"

Charlie turned to me with the amazed, revolted look of somebody who'd just felt a ghost pass through him. "Scare me? Nah, Bear. Ain't scared o' you."

His daddy was probably a drunk, many of the Deep-ins were, holed up in their houseboats in the green shade of giant trees. Some of the older Deep-ins were legendary bullies, as mean as the wild hogs they lived on. They may even have been monsters too, doling out abuse and beatings from time to time. It looked like Charlie had it worse than most. To Tom and Lester and the butcher nurses, Charlie was just another swamp critter and they were here to keep the animals in line. If they broke us, we'd obey. They didn't reckon our world was already tough enough. I guessed Charlie had just finished the last spotty year of formal education he'd ever have. Next winter, while I sat in a warm classroom, he'd likely be in the cold woods trapping foxes with his old man and taking a beating if the traps were empty. "Go get some water, kid," I said softly. He nodded and went to the faucet.

He was grinning as he walked back to the group, flashing a wide gap between his front teeth. Tap water glistened on his chin and in the hollow of his chest. He twitched from adrenaline like the rest of us, and it made him talkative. Charlie was more gregarious than most Deep-ins. He wiped his mouth down his arm in a long swipe from wrist to elbow and said, "Far's they think, we jus bad from the get-go and ain't nothin can change they minds." His quaint language tumbled out. "Dis ain't bout the lice. Bigger'n dat. Dey sent the worse deputies, dat nut cruncher Tom, and tittie squeezer Lester. Took our shirts to shame us. Took our shoes so's we can't hide nothin in em and can't run, but dey wrong, we can run and hide in the swamp like gators amongst the logs."

He looked toward the line of swamp trees where the running boys, Blaise and Nick, had disappeared. "Dey got a list o' girl names too, I seen it. Tomorrow Lester'll try to round em up and feel em up and watch em get shaved bald whilst he rubs his baton on his pecker, but he ain't gonna get off cause he won't be able to find no girls. Girls'll take to the swamp and blend in like gators." Charlie ran his hand over his head. "Know what? I bet we ain't even got the lice."

I growled, "Gonna come a time Tom Thumb won't be able to touch me no more. Sumbitch tries, I'll rip him in two and feed him to the swamp."

Charlie spread his gap-tooth grin. "Ah Bear, it coulda been worse. Hair'll grow back. I'm just glad dey didn't check me for the VD and chop somepin else off." The crowd was impressed. Some said ahhh, some laughed.

"Shit, you got VD?" I asked.

He spread bony arms. "Looka me. Think I ever got me a chance to catch the VD?"

So that's how Charlie and I began, because he was too frail to do anything but befriend. In the swampland, friendship was delicate, fluid, and provisional. Getting by was paramount, and sometimes survival was incompatible with camaraderie. Where continued existence was concerned, a friend was a luxury, but on the day they shaved our heads we were bolstered by the unifying experience of a mass indignity. The bunch of us stood laughing with a stranger, a Deep-in boy, something we would never have done under ordinary circumstances. I stretched my arms over my head and whooped like a wild man. Several boys whooped along with me.

"*La terre tremblante,* Bear," Charlie said in his quaint, sing-song Cajun. "We so bad, the ground shake."

Dehumanization, the brutality of shearing and stigma of poverty, an unforgiving swamp, our bleak prospects, were nothing to us. Stigma was a device of man; we were nature boys. The butchers thought they'd beat us down, but we were down already, weeds growing right out of the dirt, so up was the only direction for Charlie and me, and the Foley twins, and all the fellows, even the running boys, Blaise Antoine and Nick. Those two waded out of the swamp like supermen two days later, bellies filled with snake meat; the fresh hides of rabbits draped over their shaved heads.

La terre tremblante. The ground shakes, yes indeed.

Charlie had been right about one thing; our hair grew back. A year later, we all had hair hanging past our shoulders. We let it go wild and braided it like savages, just to show we could. We were all Samson, with strength and rebellion growing right out of our scalps. We thought we posed a danger to the world, and we did as we pleased. We had no idea that our misguided choices would stick to our skins and mistakes would have a way of turning permanent and aging along with us. One by one, we became what we were destined to be.

AFTER HIGH SCHOOL, I took a pass on joining the army. At the urging of my father, I applied for student loans and went to college on the government's dime. I landed a job as a baseball coach at the local high school in St. Bernard, and since then, I've been honing my writing skills at night. Some distant summer, during my time off, I'll produce the novel that'll make me rich and famous, as soon as I find the perfect blood level of bourbon to render me inspired. It's only a matter of thinking outside the box, as they say, that sly old trap of a box.

Maybe I'll write about the swampland and send those ghosts into the world, so they'll leave me alone at night. I'll tell about a cop's hand sliding up the inside of my leg, while I'm dreading what comes next, so much that my nuts pull up into my body. I'll describe the loathing and disgust that I let it happen again and again because helplessness was a coward's excuse. I'll write about the shame in my girl's eyes when the monster slid his fingers inside her panties and asked her if she liked it.

Some nights, when the summer moon's full and I'm more than a little drunk, I think about that girl's sad, pleading eyes. I remember how Lester would walk around to the passenger side and open the car door and tell her to get out. She'd turn her eyes to me, wanting me to do something to stop it, even though she knew I wouldn't. Then I'd see the mask of resignation drop over her face as she climbed out of the car, because all the while she realized that a monster, a true gator amongst the logs, was waiting for her up by the front fender.

Somewhere in that bottle, just before the blessing of boozy sleep, I see a cluster of hairless boys around a faucet, creatures of swagger and huff, no shoes or shirts, our whole lives in front and coming at us. We believed fate could be tricked; we were convinced that everything good was yet to happen for us. Given our prospects, some of us might well become bitter monsters down the line. In the meantime, for bottom dogs like us, the only direction was up. On that day we were more than bayou mongrels. We were great beasts of hope and delusion; cocky, fleeting, terrified, molded from swamp mud in God's fist and turned loose to rock the peace of the natural world.

BEAR, PART TWO:
WHAT THE DOG SAID

"If animals could speak, the dog
would be a blundering outspoken fellow. . ."
~Mark Twain

THERE WAS A season in our youth when Charlie LaForce and I grew our hair long like savages and never ran a comb through it. We let it fan out in a rebellious corona that trapped leaves and sticks and the brittle bodies of dead mosquitoes and flies. Sometimes, we braided it and wove it full of feathers. We dipped our fingers in swamp mud and drew long, drying lines across our foreheads and cheekbones. We broke open an ink pen and taped a needle to a stick and dipped the point in the ink and poked and pierced each other's bleeding backs to create two matching crude tattoos of a skull that leered at the civilization we so arrogantly shunned.

We thought we showed humanity a thing or two, but as it happened, nobody noticed, at least nobody who said so, because the wide world beyond our flood plain was blandly indifferent to a couple of scruffy, self-important posers. We only impressed each other, and just barely.

The hair, the strutting, the nose-thumbing and tattoos, all happened twenty years ago, and it happened yesterday, because those twenty years faded like a sunset. I know now that time is abstract, a matter of perception. When I first open my eyes from a night of bourbon sleep, I'm a blameless child once more in my innocent blankets, no regrets, no pain. It seems that way for a few seconds, until I move to get out of bed. That's when I perceive every single year, in every joint of my ill-used body.

I haven't held a hand mirror and contorted my spine to look at the skull on my back for, well, a very long time. That leering grin rides a generous layer of fat now. Both Charlie and I lost our hair early too, as though Mother Nature paid us back for the bug-filled manes of our youth. I miss my hair. There's only so much a comb-over can do. When I rub Charlie's head for luck, I'm stroking a bald spot, brown as a nut from the sun, and when he gives my back a lucky pounding, it sends fat waves that make my tattoo ripple like a hula girl.

Charlie's drunken, abusive old man died long ago, and so did my own loving father. The loamy soil of our homeland swallowed them both impartially and left us grieving or at peace, depending on the legacy. Now, Charlie's the only decent constant in my life. We live side by side in a couple of mobile homes in the finest trailer park in St. Bernard Parish. Of course, "fine" is a comparative term and subject to change. When things aren't so fine any more, we'll pick up and roll away. We really rent a couple of concrete pads with sewer hook-up and a power pole, and that's easy enough to switch out, when things go south.

This is a noisy neighborhood, I'll admit, but we're parked at the end of the lane where it's quieter, fewer domestics with cops busting heads, less noisy kids, more room for Charlie's junk cars in the long grass out by the back fence. We'll work up the energy to get those cars running, one of these days.

Queen Mavis runs the rental office up front. I like to watch her round ass in tight skirts. Hell, they don't charge extra for looking at Mavis, so I look plenty. I've got no woman to please since my ex-wife Lois moved out and left me alone in the trailer we once shared, in the same way two lions share a cage—lots of growling and little tolerance, and every now and then, a hell of a scrap. Then, here come the cops again.

When Lois drove away for the last time, she took my good car and left me with the old truck and this house trailer. She dropped her big butt into the driver's seat and I haven't seen her since. Just as well, I was sick of brawling all the time, and never laughing. Lois was a fair cook, but she had no sense of humor. A humorless woman is a miserable companion, and casseroles can't make up for it. I'll admit I felt only relief when she drove away, even though it was in my good car. I haven't replaced the car or the wife, and I don't plan on it. Now, when I get lonely, I just rent-to-own. It's the same way I got my new TV.

Things are different next door at Charlie's place. He likes his wife, but that's due to long distance. He's alone a lot since his wife has a job that keeps her on the road for weeks at a time. She comes home only now and then. Any two people could get along under those conditions. You forget about the bad habits, the imposition, the noise and irritation. Memory is gentle to us in that way, so to Charlie's mind, she's fine as wine when she shows up. Charlie's so glad to see her that he throws open the door and yanks her inside and poles her with the dial set on ten. The whole trailer park hears it because he's a grunter and she's a squealer. The sound is like a bullfrog crawling down a pig's throat. I'm not kidding.

First time it happened, it drew a small crowd, thinking they were hearing another bloody domestic. Even Mavis from the front office shuffled down on her high heels, so I stepped outside real quick. There were beads of sweat on her cleavage and in her puffy hair and I couldn't look away. She brushed her wet bangs aside, shifted her chewing gum and said, "Damn, Bear, what's going on in there is either awful bad or awful good."

We were about to call the cops to find out if it was bad or good when Charlie and his missus threw open the door and walked out in saturated bliss, hand-in-hand, so I guess it was awful good. He was grinning and she looked moony and ruffled. They stumbled into Charlie's old Ford, eyes only for each other, not a bit curious as to why all of us were standing in the road. She slid over on that bench seat and crowded against him, and they headed out to the diner to settle the appetite they'd worked up. I'll admit I was jealous. I've never had sexual harmony in my life, not to the extent that it left me oblivious. From the sight of them, I imagine they stuck to the seat.

I felt sorry for their dog. When Charlie and his wife opened the door, Lucky Jack bolted out and slid under the trailer, pushing and scratching with his hind legs like a dog chased by bees. I dropped down on all fours and peeked into the shadows and saw Lucky Jack flat on the dirt with his snout on his paws, shifting his wet sad eyes to give me a look of desperation. When Charlie gets busy, he should put Lucky Jack outside, show some respect for the dog. My grandpa said dogs are blessed creatures because you can say anything to a dog and he'll keep it a secret. Grandpa said someday dogs will be given the gift of speech and they'll tell us the wisdom of the ages, and some will even tell jokes. I hope so. We need wisdom and we need jokes.

I love jokes. I like to make funny things happen, especially to Charlie. Recently, I went too far at Charlie's expense, but once it got rolling, I didn't want to stop. When it all went bad, I couldn't stop it, even though I tried. How was I to know? I needed a laugh because it was raining and I was on the wagon again, cross as a rattlesnake, and so bored I could've pounded my head on the ground. Bad weather, bad everything. We'll just say the whole thing was an accident of climate, some toxic humidity, a barometric tragedy.

It started innocently, it really did. I simply strolled into the diner early that morning to get out of the rain and I found Charlie hovering over coffee in a back booth like one of the thunder clouds outside had floated through the door and stalled over his head. His clothes were crinkled on his skinny frame and his fringe of hair hung in tangled strands. That was Charlie, a janitor's mop, just a bunch of limp gray strings.

"Morning, Charlie. You look like hell. What's the matter?"

He squinted. "Oh . . . Bear. Hower ya?"

"Fine, just fine." I bought coffee and carried it to his booth. "Mind if I sit?"

He said, "Just as soon ya didn't. Need to think, me."

I put my knuckles on the table and leaned in. "Don't want company?"

"Rather not, if it be all the same."

I slid into the booth anyway. "Why don't you tell old Bear what's wrong?"

"Nothin wrong."

I propped forward on my elbows. "Well then, why you acting like this?"

He shook his head. "Ain't actin like nothin."

With Charlie, it always takes time. Somewhere along the line he lost that steely bravery he had when we were boys. He lived through a childhood nobody should endure, and never complained. Now he worries and whines. Whaa whaa whaa, until you'd rather be sitting on an ant hill. He reminds me of my ex, Lois. Never marry a woman you just met, especially if you're drunk at the ceremony. If I'd known she was such a sour puss, I could've saved myself alimony, which I stopped paying, by the way. Let the gloomy bitch sue me, what's she gonna get? My trailer? My rent-to-own TV?

I waited for Charlie to open up, just like always. People came into the diner and placed orders and left with Styrofoam boxes and paper sacks. We sat quietly, listening to rain patter against the asphalt parking lot. The reflection of raindrops running down the window looked like water squiggles moving across the tabletop. Charlie watched the water patterns.

At last, he spoke up. "Saw somepin spooky yesterday, me. You reckon it just might be the sign?"

"Sign? What sign?"

I thought about signs, a big red stop sign, a triangle yield sign, a sign with a leaping stag, *Deer Crossing*, the sign over the urinal, *All Employees Must Wash Hands*, a sign Mavis hangs on the office door with a happy face and *Be Right Back*. Most of the time she's gone two hours getting a manicure or getting a tooth filled or getting laid.

We heard a screech in the parking lot as some punk wheeled away. Charlie jumped and said, "Dunno if I oughta tell anybody bout the sign, Bear."

"Why not? You're a free man."

"Free?" he asked and pulled his mouth down on one side and gave a bitter laugh, Ha! And then, Ha! Ha! I never saw sense in laughing when something's not funny. I don't laugh at things that aren't funny and I don't abide people who do. It had been many years since Charlie lived deep in the swamp, but superstition pumped through the veins of the Deep-in people. It was their heritage, and those beliefs rested on a prescribed course with a delicate balance. Rituals were narrow and tight. Charlie was correct. A life conducted according to superstitions wasn't free, not at all.

He said, "Ain't free no more since I seen it. Might be the sign and now I'm the only one can do somepin bout it."

I asked, "Nobody else saw this sign, whatever it was?"

"Jus myself . . . and Lucky Jack."

I turned up both hands. "So what was the sign?"

Charlie drew a deep breath. "Well, see, my brother, he ast me to go in half on a breeder boar. Can't pay for the whole hog by hisself."

I grinned. "If you buy half, buy the back half. The front half has to be fed."

"Huh?"

"Forget it."

He continued, "I reckoned if I oughta or not, so my wife, she told me to ast God for a sign." It made sense that Charlie's wife would turn to God for an answer. She'd screamed His name in that trailer enough times.

I was suddenly on unfamiliar ground. Religion has always been a mystery to me. I have a distorted picture of God, like a Picasso face with eyes askew and a nose where an ear should be, so I fell back on what I did know: God has a sense of humor. He made that weirdo Picasso, didn't He? Sometimes, God does things because they're funny, and when God cooks a joke, it's bound to be epic, so I wanted in on it.

"What happened, Charlie? Just tell it. You can trust me, buddy."

He took a deep breath and told me his spooky story about the sign. When he was finished he asked me to keep it to myself but I knew it would be impossible. I was part of a joke that was unwinding from God's fingertips and I had to act. Besides, it would be funny, really funny.

I drank my coffee in big gulps, stood up, and for tradition's sake, I slid my hand over Charlie's bald spot. He absentmindedly reached and pounded my back a couple of times. Then he went back to brooding. I was zinging with the excitement a comedian must feel when a good joke is spinning in his brain. I left the diner to spread Charlie's story around.

I decided to set up my base of operations in Billy's Tavern next door to the diner.

When I walked into Billy's, there was an old codger on a bar stool with his head on the bar, sleeping. Billy (Howdy! Welcome to

Billy's!) was at his usual post behind the bar, wiping around the old drunk's head. Billy's a burly short fellow who believes if he talks loud it will give him the illusion of height.

Two regulars were at a table with breakfast beers. I slid onto a bar stool and watched Billy wiping around the drunk. The old man snored softly with his face on his hand. His huge nose gaped down the bar at me, and it was like peering into a two-car garage. I was on the wagon, so I ordered a Diet Coke and black coffee and Billy slid them in front of me.

"Here ya go, Bear!"

Billy had seen me fumble and drop many attempts at sobriety. He had a bartender's understanding of crawling on the wagon and falling off at the first bump in the road, so he knew I'd hit the roadbed pretty soon and he accepted it without judgment. It's a comfort to be accepted, a blessing to be un-judged.

I quietly sipped the Coke and coffee, alternating hot and cold, and thought about the strange story Charlie had told me. He said that he'd been riding in his Ford yesterday with Lucky Jack on the back seat. The dog was looking out the window, drooling like always, and that's when it happened. Charlie was so shocked that he swerved to the side of the road, laying a zigzag skid of rubber.

Charlie had said, "Bear, somebody in the back seat done said somepin."

"Who?"

Charlie shrugged. "Musta been Lucky Jack. Hadda be. Weren't but him back dere."

"Lucky Jack said real people words? Not dog noises?"

Charlie threw up his hands. "See dat? I knew nobody'd believe me."

"I believe you. Just tell me what happened. What, exactly, did the dog say?"

Charlie glanced around, leaned closer to me, and whispered, "Mama."

"Mama? For real?"

"Right hand to God Almighty." He crossed himself and kissed his thumb.

Charlie said when he'd heard the voice from the back seat, he jumped out of the car and stood looking through the window, trying to find a person back there. Lucky Jack looked blandly through the window at his master. Charlie opened the car door and eased into the driver's seat. By that time, he doubted his own ears, so he sat behind the wheel until he built up his nerve, then he turned and studied the dog like a scholar reading an ancient map.

"I ast Lucky Jack, 'You say dat, boy? You say Mama?' but he wouldn't say it, no, not to my face. Dat damn dog, he wait til I was turn around front, den he say it to my back again. I swear he did, Bear. He—say—Mama."

By way of clarification, Charlie said it sounded like *maaah-mah*, like a drunk might say it with a mouth full of slime, but it was still a word from a critter that had no business making conversation. Charlie tried to get Lucky Jack to say it a third time, three times the charm. "Do dat again, boy, jus one mo time. Say it while I'm watchin."

Lucky Jack drooled.

Then louder, "C'mon, boy, say Mama again!"

The dog looked out the window.

"Say dat again!"

Lucky Jack lifted a hind leg and scratched behind his ear.

Charlie begged and Lucky Jack listened politely, then after what seemed to be a spell of intelligent thought, the dog folded up on the seat and fell asleep.

"He say it twice in the car, I swear, but jus when I wasn't lookin."

"Hell, Charlie, that dog could make you rich!"

"But what if he don never say it again? People, dey won't believe me. Like I say, never seen him do it, me, but I heard. And the friggin dog, he keep on doin it."

"What do you mean?"

Charlie said he'd been reading under the covers that night with Lucky Jack curled on the foot of the bed like always. Charlie clicked off the light, and from the darkness:

Maah-mah

Charlie clicked on the light and stared at the dog, but Lucky Jack pretended to be asleep.

Next morning, Charlie had a frying pan in hand, spooning scrambled eggs onto a plate when Lucky Jack came into the kitchen. Behind Charlie:

Maah-mah

Charlie was so startled that he spilled eggs on the floor.

"Done it on purpose, to vex me, dat sumbitch dog," he told me. Charlie was so upset that he ran outside. Last thing he heard before he slammed the door was the sound of Lucky Jack slurping scrambled eggs off the linoleum. Charlie drove to the diner, and that's where I found him and heard his story.

At Billy's bar, Billy refilled my Coke and coffee. I had to whiz twice over the next hour, but gradually the crowd grew to a respectable number of regulars. I waited until the time was perfect. Poor timing can ruin a good joke. At last, with the skill of a professional, I cleared my throat and cracked my knuckles. It was time to let the cat—or in this case the dog—out of the bag.

Loud enough for the whole bar to hear, I said, "Billy, you lived round here a long time. You ever hear Charlie LaForce's dog say anything?"

There's something about the start of a good joke that changes the air in a room. It feels like static on your skin. Energy moves through the pit of your gut and zips up your throat and makes you giggle and breathe faster. I felt this kind of change move over the crowd in the bar. They stopped talking and started listening, on alert, their guts and throats tight with anticipation. Even Old Man Nostrils lifted his head and paid attention.

Billy stopped wiping. "You mean Lucky Jack? What you trying to say, Bear?"

I repeated the question. "Ever hear Lucky Jack talk?"

Billy relaxed and grinned. "Bear, you pulling my leg?"

Another thing about Billy; he's always answers a question with a question. He was doing it to me and it threw off my timing and made me cross. I could've done with a more cooperative straight man.

"I'm not pulling anything of yours, Billy," I snapped. "I'm serious as Geronimo."

Then I layered it on, adding words and weight, which amounts to truth in some guy's minds. "Look, all cards on the table, fellows, right hand to God, trust me on this. I was told, just this very morning, by a completely sober fellow, that Lucky Jack talks."

Laughing, Billy yelled, "Who told you that?"

"Charlie LaForce, himself."

When I said Charlie's name, everybody guffawed and slapped their knees. Billy said, "Well Bear, you reckon Charlie might've been a little drunk at the time?"

I should've told them that Charlie didn't drink near as much as the guys who were laughing at him for being drunk, but I didn't say it. I didn't say anything good and I didn't feel anything bad. I simply let the joke spin out. It's criminal to stop a good joke before its time.

Billy said, "That dog's a German something-or-other. Does it talk German or does it talk English?" The bar guys were loving it.

"Yeah, the dog talks—uh, *speaks*—English, for your information. He keeps saying Mama, but only when Charlie's not looking. Charlie thinks it might be a miracle."

Billy said, "Yeah, maybe, if it were true, which I doubt. Miracles are rare for guys like us. Drunken delusions, on the other hand, ain't rare a-tall."

The old man at the end of the bar asked, "When did Charlie and Lucky Jack have these conversations?"

"They weren't conversations. Lucky Jack only says one word, now and then, when Charlie's not looking."

The old man laughed and said, "Lucky Jack only says one word now and then, huh? Damn! He'd make a good wife."

More chuckles.

Billy drummed his fingers on the bar. Finally, he asked, "Bear, where'd you see Charlie last?"

"Next door at the diner, but that was a couple hours ago."

The door swung open and Wilson Fox walked into the bar with his little son Everett. Wilson was prone to a mid-morning nip, and his wife mistakenly thought she could prevent it by making Wilson take Everett on his outings, but Wilson had found a way around having a five-year-old chaperone. Wilson simply plopped Everett on a bar stool and fed the boy beer nuts from the bowl with the stipulation that Everett not tell his mama where they'd been. It was an admirable plan, masculine, almost perfect, as long as Everett didn't eat too many nuts and get sick. Wilson always counted out the appropriate ration and cut Everett off with much more resolve than he practiced on himself.

Wilson was counting nuts for Everett when the group decided to send the boy next door to the diner to see if Charlie was still there. Everett left and shortly reported back that Charlie was not to be found.

I said, "He's been working overtime down at the fire station. Must've gone home to rest. Let sleeping dogs lie, so to speak. Better leave him be, boys."

The boys didn't agree. "I wanna hear that dog talk," said Old Man Nostrils. "Yeah, let's bring him in here and make him say something," said one of the breakfast beers.

"Anybody up for a little wager?" asked the gin and tonic at the back of the room.

At that moment I realized that there was a problem with this particular joke. No exit plan. The situation was gaining momentum and I didn't have a way to cut it off. It's funny when something goes out of control. Funny, that is, except to the person who can't keep things in check.

I tried to reel it in. "Joke's over, fellows." I was ignored.

Wilson Fox said, "Billy, if you'll lend me your car, I'll drive over to Charlie's trailer and bring him back, and the dog too. You got to watch Everett, though. Just don't let him eat too many nuts."

Billy fished in his pocket for his keys and tossed them to Wilson and said, "Wait a minute, Wilson, don't want dog drool in the car!" He gave Wilson a bar apron to tie around Lucky Jack's neck. Wilson left to fetch Charlie and Lucky Jack.

Word spread fast. I blame the advent of cell phones. Everybody in the bar held one to his ear and the bar filled in fifteen minutes. I couldn't believe it. No, wait . . . I had no problem at all believing it. I'd done this kind of thing before. I knew the exact role that human nature plays in a joke. Everything's funnier when it's shared. Soon, the bar stools were full, all the tables too. Billy pulled beers and yelled "Howdy!" until he was hoarse. We ran out of room in the bar, so the benches on the sidewalk outside filled and guys sat on the curb, smoking, teasing, and knuckle-punching shoulders. In about thirty minutes, Wilson came back with Charlie. Lucky Jack trotted into the bar between them wearing the apron, damp with drool. Charlie looked scared and miserable.

Wilson said, "Charlie—here—he was expecting me, or somebody like me, to come fetch him. He got to thinking he told Bear—here—too much, so it was only a matter of time before somebody showed up because he didn't expect Bear to keep his promise to stay quiet."

Charlie said, "Yeah, figure I better come clear things up fore Bear do too much damage."

Charlie might know me very well, but I knew more about people in general than Charlie did. I realized the crowd in the bar didn't care if the talking dog was a miracle or a sign from God or the Apocalypse in neon lights. All they wanted was a freak show.

There was bumping and scraping as the crowd moved tables to clear the center of the room for the big show. Early morning rain had blown over and sunlight came through the front window and cast backward lettering of the bar's name on the floor where Charlie and Lucky Jack stood. The crowd outside suddenly blocked sunlight as they pressed against the window to get a look. Billy stepped into the cleared space and held up his hand to command silence. Fellows in the back of the crowd goose-necked and shushed each other.

Billy shouted, "Charlie, a man has to be really old—or really rich—to run his mouth without apology, okay? You ain't old and you ain't rich neither, but you been running your mouth anyway, claiming Lucky Jack talks, right? Claim like that has to be backed up, else you make fools of us all, know what I mean? Now you gonna prove it, or what?"

Charlie swallowed and locked eyes with me for a second before he looked away. "Yeah Billy, Lucky Jack, he talk a few times, but don't know if I can prove it. Maybe he do it again for strangers, maybe he not. Don't care either way, me, cause it was a sign from God, and I see it now."

"A sign from God?" Billy yelled for the crowd. "Well, if my name ain't Billy, huh?" Then he spelled it for us, "Bee...eye...ale...

ale…why!"

The crowd laughed. I never realized how commanding Billy was, what a great humorist. It would be a valuable asset for a bartender to make people laugh, and make them happy for a little while. Of course, flowing booze would help.

Charlie closed his eyes against the laughter. But then he felt a gentle tug on his sleeve and looked down into the blue eyes of little Everett Wilson. "Mr. Charlie, can you get him to talk again?"

Little Everett had said "again." The five-year-old seemed to be the only believer in the crowd. I think the boy's trust comforted Charlie because he was, after all, a child-like man, himself. Charlie must've seen a reflection of his own innocent faith and uncomplicated purity. He'd been a boy who believed a simple touch on the back could give another boy courage. He regularly conducted joyous, noisy, unselfconscious sex with his wife and one-word conversations with his dog. He grew up with soul-crushing abuse, but kept his trust in mankind's benevolence. On the ground floor, he was as straightforward as a man could be, including his hope for a miracle that involved a temperamental, tricky critter that refused to fully disclose a marvelous aberration.

Charlie said, "Old Cajun sayin, Everett. *Les attrapes sont mises pour les innocents.* It mean for the innocent, dere are many traps. Dis dog, he know dat, and he scared of dem traps, even around me, and he trust me pretty good. Dat's why I ain't never really seen him talk. Only heard him."

Billy interrupted, "Look, LaForce, there's a hell of a lot of difference between innocent and gullible. We're not gullible and we're not fools. We're waiting for you to back up what you been claiming."

Everett looked up at Charlie. "They just want to hear him too, like you did. Don't be afraid, neither one of you." The boy reached and ran his hand gently over Lucky Jack's head, just as I had so often slid the palm of my hand over Charlie's head, as though Charlie were my pet. I hadn't realized before, not in all those years, what a condescending gesture it was, and how demeaning.

"You right, Everett, they wanna hear too." Charlie sighed in resignation.

I heard Charlie's knees pop as he squatted in front of Lucky Jack. The room fell quiet and the crowd on the street hushed. Little Everett stepped up close to Charlie and laid his small hand on Charlie's shoulder in a gesture of comfort. Charlie took Lucky Jack's face in his hands and the dog's jowls folded over his fingers. He looked into Lucky Jack's eyes.

"C'mon, say mama for old Charlie, won't cha, boy?"

Dog drool ran in silver strings through Charlie's fingers and down the apron.

Charlie tried again. "You can do it boy, talk to Charlie."

The crowd grumbled and Billy yelled another question. "Well Charlie, can he talk or can't he?"

Everett's hand squeezed Charlie's shoulder—*don't give up.*

As I watched Everett make this innocent gesture of support, I wondered if the Big Hair missionary ladies were responsible for the child's unquestioning faith, his belief in an impossible phenomenon. Had they done us all such an injustice when they taught us, the whole room full of us, to hope beyond all reservation for the grossly improbable?

Don't give up.

Charlie looked back at Everett, and I saw Charlie's face relax, as though he'd had a comforting idea, but when he spoke to Everett, I knew it wasn't an idea that had come to Charlie, it was a memory. He told the boy, "Know what, Everett? Lucky Jack, he hidin like a gator amongst the logs, like us boys did, back when we hide in the swamp from them mean old nurses and deputies. You never gonna see a gator in the logs until he ready for you to see, and you only hear what he want you to hear. I gotta trick um, make um give hisself away." Charlie winked at Everett.

To Lucky Jack, Charlie said, "Boy, you been talkin like a man, now a man gonna howl like a dog." Charlie took a breath, threw back his head, and slid down a winding history to our bayou ancestors; gator hunters who'd lived in harmony with the earth's vilest creatures. From Charlie's throat poured a piercing howl that brought up gooseflesh across the crowd.

"AAARRR-r-r-r Wooo Wooo Wooo-o-o-o."

Charlie looked at the dog and said, "Dat's the best I got, boy. Your turn now. No more you hide, c'mon out." Lucky Jack agreed, I suppose, because he looked Charlie in the eye and said it.

Maah-mah

The place exploded.

Lucky Jack had spoken clear and loud and perfect. There'd be no argument that it was a genuine word, one of the most treasured words in any man's language, and it came from the mouth of a dog, and a trailer park dog, at that.

Charlie rubbed Lucky Jack's head and ruffled his ears until they danced around his head. He rose to his feet and everybody pressed close to slap him on the back and shake his hand, slick with dog drool. Charlie grinned his gap-toothed grin and worked his way through the crowd until he found me.

He said, "Don worry bout it, Bear. All living things follow dey nature. You make promises you can't keep and you don't understand why, but keepin promises ain't in you nature, never was. You the same as Lucky Jack. You can't help it. You one of the *les innocents* cause you jus being what you are." Then he gave me a pat between my shoulder blades.

That did it. He'd done me in. I was prepared for anything except forgiveness. I couldn't brace for an ending like that, not in a lifetime. Maybe I was one of the innocents, like Charlie said, following my nature, but my nature was to be a cur, bully, villain, liar, false friend. I wasn't entitled to the clemency Charlie gave me. I took it, but I hadn't earned it.

I slipped out the door, jumped in my car, drove home, fell off the wagon, and hit the roadbed. With booze came the astringent clarity that my trailer had become my fate, a box filled with stale divorced air, a place where I was the gator, blending in until I disappeared and became part of the pipes and concrete steps and plastic skirting. Next door was Charlie's trailer, his arena of a life lived well with his wife and his dog and his belief in miracles. I stung with bitterness and jealousy. I had no affectionate wife, no loyal pet. I had no gape-toothed smile. I had no rainbow luck. I'd turned my back on the fact that anything's possible, but Charlie lived with that creed every glorious day, in the innocent bliss of unbridled belief.

Two hours later, I watched somebody bring Charlie and Lucky Jack home. In my drunken miasma, I noticed they were in fine spirits, man and dog, and I loved and hated them with a sot's ambiguity.

I SPENT DRUNKEN days hiding in my trailer, languishing in my fall to rock bottom, savoring my penitent misery and my friendless solitude. Queen Mavis walked down and knocked on my door, but I didn't respond. I thought she was motivated by concern for me, but no, the rent was due. She taped the bill to my door. She'd drawn a smiley face on it. I grinned when I saw that simple bit of cheer. (Ah, there you are, my sense of humor.) Oh, Mavis, Mavis, what am I doing to myself? Moreover, what could I do with you?

I crawled out of hiding. I twisted and moved to ease the stiffness in my joints, fried some eggs, opened the windows, cleaned up the place, showered and shaved. I called Mavis and told her to come down and get the rent and anything else she wanted from good old Bear. She laughed when I told her to put the smiley face sign on her door because I had a tattoo she might want to see. She said *hummm . . . okay*, and I knew we'd be all right. Shyness was never my problem, or hers. I'd show her the tattoo and all the rest of Bear and things would work out for both of us. Afterward, she'd tell me how good it was, and I'd believe her because I needed to believe in something even if wasn't true. I was done with the belly-crawl through self-pity. I've always hated a whiner.

Next morning, I met Charlie for breakfast at the diner. He told me Lucky Jack hadn't uttered another word but that was okay. It was still a miracle in Charlie's opinion, so he cast his lot with chance. He called his brother and went in halves on the breeder hog. His brother joked that Charlie could have the front half because that's the end that had to be fed. Charlie told me it reminded him of something he'd already heard, but he couldn't recall who'd said it. "Come to think of it, ain't even sure I really heard it."

He confessed that the comment may have been only inside his

head, like those spirit voices we all hear in the moments before we slide into sleep. He admitted he could've made it up, a misty dream of a hog divided across the middle, front part and rear trotting down the road, literally side by side. As far as my innocent friend knew, those words . . . *buy the back half*. . . could've been a catchy line from a country song, or a secret whispered in his ear long ago, or a sound bounced off the hills, an echo that rode the cold night air through his bedroom window, stirred the curtains as it passed, and melted in the warmth of his sleeping breath.

THE ALEKHINE DEFENSE IN FOUR

"Dogs never bite me. Just humans."
~Marilyn Monroe

IN THE FIRST half of the twentieth century, an unknown Russian named Alexander Alekhine emerged from a chessboard in the same way that Venus rose from the sea, fully realized and breathtaking. To this day, Alekhine is regarded as one of the ten best chess players in the history of the game: fierce, imaginative, merciless.

Over the course of his lifetime, two world wars had raged around him, taking the lives of millions of his countrymen, but Alekhine drew strength from the turmoil. As a young lad during World War I, and a mature man in World War II, he studied the attacking movements of conquering armies. Using borrowed military genius, he gained revolutionary insight into the art of baffling an opponent.

Alekhine's strength wasn't in his knowledge of chess moves. It was, instead, his cultured understanding of the human psyche and its desire for balance and orderliness. Man's need for organization was a vulnerability that Alekhine used to his advantage as he developed his opening attack, the Alekhine Defense. With the first four moves, he cluttered the center of the board with pawns, throwing off the symmetry of the game and turning his opponent's need for harmony into a weapon. He thrived in the resulting chaos.

The first time Alekhine ever spoke to me, he'd been dead for sixty-seven years. Naturally, his voice was quite unexpected.

Alice, Alice Smiley, go look in the mirror.
"Who said that?"
I've taken something of yours, Alice. Go look in the mirror, in the mirror.

I knew it was Alekhine, even though I'd never heard his voice, not even in a scratchy recording or jerky old newsreel. Sometimes I could recognize the voices, and sometimes not, but I was sure this new voice was his. It wasn't the Boris-and-Natasha Russian accent that made me so sure. My confidence came from a lifetime of anticipation. I was twenty-five years old, and I'd been waiting for Alekhine all my life, even during my episodes of heaviest medication.

Schizophrenia is manageable with drugs, they say. Ah, but there's the rub, those terrible, numbing drugs. Imagine standing on two sides of a prison door, both at once. Part of you is out and free, but part's walled up in an isolating cell of medication, like a crazy relative locked away in the attic. Two sides of you are screaming the truth, but they're at odds, contradictory, and both sides swear they're not lying.

Alekhine's voice had a soothing, caressing quality, almost romantic:

Alice, I've taken something of yours, something of yours. Go look in the mirror.

Look in the mirror.

I went obediently to the mirror over the bathroom vanity.

At first glance, everything seemed to be in place, until I pulled back my hair and discovered that my left ear had vanished from the side of my head, neat as a Quaker.

I've taken something of yours. Something of yours.

Some.

Thing.

In my reflection, the left side of my head continued from front to back in an unbroken plane, as earless as a turtle's noggin.

Even more strange, my earring dangled unsupported in midair, suspended in space like a magician's prop, an inch from the bend of my jaw. I could touch my ear, despite all visual evidence. My fingers slid smoothly over the unseen scallop of skin and cartilage and found the place where the simple shiny hoop passed through the pliable earlobe.

"Far out, Alekhine," I whispered, so my husband Jack couldn't hear.

I fingered the warm circle of silver, poked my finger through it, shook my head and watched it jiggle. I could see the whole and unbroken ring.

"The ear's a neat trick sir, and the earring's a clever touch."

And then, Jack shouted from the dining room, "Are you going to take all night, Alice? I'm hungry!"

"Just a minute, Jack!"

I rummaged through a drawer and found my hand mirror. I turned to examine my profile and saw an ear-shaped hole all the way through my head, like a keyhole in a door. Looking through the hole, I saw the shower curtain behind me; little sailboats and sea gulls like flattened vees and a squiggle of painted waves.

"Very thorough job," I said to Alekhine.

Jack again. "ALICE SMILEY! GET IN HERE!"

I knew Jack would be sitting at the table with his knife in one hand and his fork in the other, but he wouldn't take a bite until I was there, my butt in the chair and my elbows off the table. I hurried to the dining room and slid apologetically into my chair.

Jack began to eat in his prissy way, everything devoured in democratic proportions so that it all came out even. He never made that chalkboard scrape of knife against plate, and when I did, he'd stop chewing and give me a dirty look every time, as though I'd done it on purpose.

"Salt," he said around a mouthful as he snapped his fingers.

I handed the salt to him and waited, not daring to mention that Alekhine was stealing parts of me. Jack would simply accuse me of being crazy again. He demanded normalcy because he was a high school principal and could get away with domination. It was his bread and butter.

Not long ago, his authority reached new heights, or, rather, new depths. I'd thrashed through a bad bout of irrationality following my father's death, watching the walls drip, my hands over my ears, screaming for the voices to stop. "Mad as a hatter," as Jack put it. He bullied my psychiatrist into putting me through a round of humiliating shock treatments. I'll never forgive him, and who can blame me?

Finally, I had to make him look at me. "How do you like my hair?"

He tilted his head one way, then the other, studying my head.

"Same as always," he said, growing suspicious. "What are you getting at? You're not turning goofy again, are you?"

In college, Jack had majored in conclusions. Evidently, he could see both ears, so Alekhine's trick was for my eyes only.

"Never mind," I said, and twirled my fork in my mashed potatoes.

He snapped, "Don't play with your food."

We never wasted food. He'd probably bring up the starving people of the world, as he always did, when I wasn't eating enough. I cut my steak and made the chalkboard sound on purpose. He gave me a dirty look so I lowered my head and ate the tasteless food, open and swallow, over and over, until I had cleaned my plate, as Jack insisted for the sake of worldwide sustenance.

As I cleared the supper dishes, I studied my reflection in the window over the sink and saw that the ear was still missing. I turned and watched Jack step into the doorway. He picked at his teeth with a pinkie nail and made sucking sounds with his lip curled.

"Don't forget to take your pill," he reminded me, as he did each night.

Immediately, Alekhine mocked Jack: *Don't forget to take your pill-l-l-l.*

I knew instantly that Alekhine hated Jack, but the feeling was justified, in my opinion. Order and routine were Alekhine's enemies. I removed a pill from the bottle and pretended to put it in my mouth. When Jack wasn't looking, I dropped it down the garbage disposal, as I'd done every night for a month.

When he moved away from the doorway, I turned up the music on the kitchen CD player, flipped the switch on the noisy disposal, leaned over the sink, and silently heaved up my supper. I was rinsing my mouth when I heard Jack's voice behind me.

"What are you playing?" he asked.

I twitched with alarm, but he was only referring to the music.

"The Village People," I answered, barely above a whisper.

"Bunch of old codger has-beens," he sneered. "They should change their name to 'The Retirement Village People.'" He chuckled at his own joke.

"They're fun, Jack, you know, YMCA and all." I sang the letters, my voice tapering away at the end: "Y-M . . . C . . . A . . ."

Jack clicked off the music and dropped the kitchen into silence. "How about a game of chess?" he asked.

"Okay, chess would be good."

He always let me play white, but even making the first move, I could never win, which was why he enjoyed our games. I played miserably that night, all the while hoping for some guidance from Alekhine, but the Russian master remained stubbornly silent as I struggled. Jack efficiently took my queen in just a few moves.

Of all the chess pieces, I've always loved the white queen. I was a child when my father taught me how extraordinary she was, how unique. I visited my father every week in the psychiatric hospital where he spent the years of my childhood. His room was a second home to me, and I crawled into bed beside him so he could read to me from Lewis Carroll's wonderful adventure *Through the Looking Glass*. The heroine, Alice, shared my name.

"Who's your favorite character in the book, Daddy?"

"Well, next to Alice, I believe it's the white queen, of course."

"Why?"

"Because everything's so difficult for her. In her backward, looking-glass world, the white queen actually lives in reverse. Any time you're feeling out of place or confused, Alice, stop and think how hard it must be in the white queen's world where all the rules are opposite of what seems natural."

After he read to me, he picked up the white queen from the chessboard with his long fingers that always smelled of pipe tobacco. "The white queen's very powerful," he said, handing the piece to me.

"More powerful than the black queen?"

"Oh yes, because white makes the first move. Offense is always better than defense. Just ask Alekhine."

"Who?" It was the first time I'd ever heard the name.

"Alexander Alekhine. Russian chess player, many, many years ago. Made his own rules for living, had a taste for older women, married them and abandoned them without warning. Simply walked out. He was outrageous and unprecedented and thrived on chaos. Famous for his four opening moves. He cluttered up the center of the board with pawns, and this threw off the symmetry of the playing field. The untidiness was devastating to other players."

"If he was famous for it, wouldn't they be expecting it?"

"Good question. I suppose they were, but the reality of the messiness was too much. You'd be surprised how disorienting it is to opponents when things aren't symmetrical. It's opposite of what's natural. It's backward, like the world of the white queen. Alekhine seemed to be building a defensive wall of pawns, but he was actually staging a brutal psychological attack. He knew if you muddle a man's mind, you can step through the cracks in his confusion and break him. Alekhine was intimidating, brilliant, and handsome. He looked like Gregory Peck."

"Gregory Peck sounds like the name of a cartoon chicken in a comic strip."

My father laughed. "There was nothing chicken about Alekhine. Once, he played 28 opponents in 28 games, all at the same time. It took hours. He won 22 of the games."

"Well, he didn't win them all."

"Humpff!" my father said. "He was blindfolded the whole time."

"Wow," I said, and never doubted Alekhine again.

The white queen rested warm and damp in my little hand. "Does the chess queen live in reverse, like the white queen in the book?"

He smiled. "Oh yes, she can move in reverse, or to the front, or to the side if she wants. She can attack from across the board. The white queen goes where she pleases."

"Why did you do that?" Jack asked, pulling me back to the present. "You've thrown away your queen and ruined the game. You're hopeless. You make it too easy."

I knew he wanted it easy. He would've been disappointed if I'd made a real effort to win.

LATER, I TOWELED off from my shower and was tugging my nightgown over my head when he came into the bathroom without knocking. He stood behind me and ran a finger down the length of my spine, like a butcher bisecting the backbone of a cow. He divided me into two neat halves that seemed to fall away to the floor on each side. I heard the airy *pommpff* as they hit the tile floor.

In the mirror, I saw Jack's face and the expression that he reserved for these occasions, so I dropped the nightgown and trudged to the bedroom. Before he followed, Jack stooped and picked up the discarded gown and folded it neatly and took a minute to put the bathroom in order. I wondered if Alekhine watched him from a dark corner of the board and took note of Jack's fondness for organization and symmetry.

THE NEXT MORNING, the first voice I heard was Alekhine's:
Go look in the mirror, Alice.
In the mirror, Alice.

I discovered that the left ear was still gone, and now the right ear, as well. Without them, my head looked like a painted face on a Grecian urn. "They're both gone," I said.

Now you can hear me perfectly, Alekhine said. Then he quoted Lewis Carroll: *Take care of the sense and the sounds will take care of themselves.*

By two o'clock I'd lost my nose. I could look all the way through my head and see the sailboat printed on the shower curtain behind me.

At three o'clock, there was a clear circle where my right eye had been.

Alekhine was slowly and methodically dissecting me, creating chaos. I was disappearing, and I knew I didn't stand a chance against a man who could play twenty-eight games without looking at a single board. I began to wonder if my hero Alekhine was truly on my side.

THE FOLLOWING DAY was Saturday, and Jack would be home all day. As usual, I was awakened by Alekhine's voice. I obeyed his order and got up to check the mirror. Still gone, all of it, and the left eye as well, which gave me a sparkling psychedelic appearance. Alekhine chuckled softly. I went outside to mulch the flowerbeds, grateful to be out of the house because Jack was inside, sorting his *Star Trek* collection.

He'd been a fan, a closet Trekkie, for years, using the spare room to display his cosmic trophies. There were models of the Starship Enterprise on plastic stands, wax Spock ears, Klingon Birds of Prey, fluffy pocket-sized Tribbles, assorted phasers, and a stolen brassiere worn by Uhura that he'd bought on eBay. He'd learned to mimic, "Beam me up, Scottie," and he'd mastered the double-fingered Spock V greeting. He talked about the virtues of warp speed, and when he got drunk at school board conventions, he ran around applying the Vulcan death grip to other high school principals.

For the rest of the day, Alekhine was silent, but that night, he spoke in my dreams.

Let's go sailing. Sailing with Alice Smiley, yes!

In my dream I was with my father on his sailboat once more. We laughed and wiped sea foam from our faces while flattened vees of shower curtain gulls screamed and plunged into the white squiggles of waves.

By Monday, my entire body was gone except for my mouth floating in the air. I opened it and saw the white pickets of my teeth, my gums and tongue, my angular gullet, my uvula. Held agape, my mouth created a pink tunnel in space. I telephoned my psychiatrist's office. Could I come in? Of course it's an emergency. When is it not?

Dr. Carpenter sat across his desk from me, pre-opinionated and mustached and mounded. "Shall we begin?" he asked.

The time has come to talk of many things, Alekhine said, quoting Lewis Carroll again. *The doctor's a walrus, Alice, yes!*

Alekhine was right. If Gregory Peck was a chicken, Dr. Carpenter was indeed a walrus. I looked at him and imagined that he had the bulbous head of a giant walrus. Of course, his skin was dark and leathery and whiskers sprouted from his snout. He smelled like rotting seaweed. His beady, watery, walrus eyes assessed me. In a professional, custard voice, his lipless mouth said, "What seems to be the problem, Alice?"

I'm not insane, really. I knew he wasn't truly a walrus, he just looked like one to Alekhine and me. I didn't think this was unusual. I accepted it as part of a healthy imagination, or perhaps a chaotic world.

I answered, "I'm disappearing. I realize I'm still here because I can feel myself, but I can't see myself. Can you see me?"

His animal eyes regarded me. I heard his long curved spine creak as he turned his neckless head. "Of course I see you."

"When I look in the mirror, there's nothing there but my mouth. It's like a magic show where I stepped into a cabinet and vanished, a piece at a time."

He drummed his flipper on the blotter. "M-m-m-m. Have you been obsessing over your father again? Do you fear you're disappearing from the world as he did?"

"Disappearing? That's a simple explanation for death."

He ignored me. "Have you told Jack about this?"

"Heavens, no! Don't even suggest it. He might send me back to that awful asylum. Jack doesn't like problems, he only likes routine."

"Well, he's correct. Routine keeps you grounded in reality. Disorder is disorienting." He smiled at his own word play. I was talking with a giant walrus. This didn't fit the definition of reality or disorder or being grounded. It simply *was*.

The walrus said, "I've explained the genetic factor of your mental illness many times. Schizophrenia runs in your family. It's gone from your father to you."

Tell him about the voices. Voices, tell him, Alice. Begin at the beginning, then go on until you come to the end; then stop.

Alekhine's thick accent came from the chair to my right. He was using Lewis Carroll's words to prompt me, but of course, in my backward world, the chair was empty.

"Hush," I whispered to the chair. "Will you please stop quoting Carroll?"

The walrus doctor asked, "What do you see, Alice? What do you hear? Are you talking to someone?"

"I see only you of course, who else is here?" I stuck out my chin.

He eyed Alekhine's empty chair. "Humph," he said, reaching

for his prescription pad with his flipper. "Alice, I'm going to give you a mild antidepressant to add to the anti-psychotic you're already taking."

"More pills? Oh no! I can't stand to be zonked any more. I only wanted a second opinion because Jack doesn't see that I'm not all there."

Doctor Carpenter pressed into his backrest. The chair groaned. "But you *are* all there."

"That's not what he says."

"Who?"

"Alekhine."

"Who's Alekhine?"

"The Russian who's not sitting in that chair." I poked a thumb at the empty chair.

Carpenter blinked his ugly walrus eyelashes. "But nobody's in that chair!"

"That's exactly what I said!" I threw my invisible hands in the air.

We're all mad here, Alekhine contributed, quoting Carroll again.

"Don't worry, Alice, you're not disappearing."

"Are you sure?"

"Yes Alice, I only see things that are there, and *you* are there."

"I see," I said.

"And what do you see?"

"I'm all there."

"Correct!"

Carpenter wrapped his flipper around a pen and scribbled on a prescription pad. "You'll find this helpful. Have it filled and everything will be fine. That's a good girl."

He tore off the square of paper and slid it to me across the desk.

"Okay," I sighed, and stuffed it into my purse.

I slipped out of his office and strolled down the sidewalk past the St. Bernard Florist Shop. There was a display of cheerful Mylar balloons in the window. "Happy Birthday" said one, in letters like a rainbow. "Congratulations" said another. "It's a Boy!" in blue, "I Love You" on a pink heart, "Bon Voyage" in silver.

Mr. Phillips, the florist, saw me through the window and stepped outside to greet me. Termites crawled all over his body and in and out of his collar. I was suddenly convinced that he hid poisonous spiders in his floral arrangements. They'd be perfect murder weapons. You could send a bouquet to your enemy, a seemingly loving gesture, but hidden inside the roses or lilies would be untraceable death. The spider would strike and skitter away, leaving chaos and disorder in its wake. I wondered if I could get away with sending flowers to Jack.

The florist said, "Hello, Mrs. Smiley. Haven't seen you for a while."

I grimaced. "That makes two of us. I haven't seen me either."

"Beg pardon?" said Mr. Phillips, as a termite skittered up one nostril.

"Never mind." I turned and hurried down the street.

I HAD SUPPER ready at six, as Jack ordered, but he was late. At nine, I pushed it down the disposal, taking delight in wasting all that food. When he showed up at midnight, I questioned his whereabouts and he slapped me. I rushed to the bedroom and sat on the bed as a red welt appeared on my cheek.

"I'm sorry," he told me, standing in the doorway. "I was at the Trekkie convention. I forgot to call, that's all. I didn't hurt you, did I? It was just a little tap."

"If my father were alive, he'd come and get me. We'd sail away and you'd never see me again. He'd take me some place safe, then he'd come after you."

"Alice, we've been over this a thousand times. Your father *is* alive, in a mental institution in Tulsa, hospitalized for schizophrenia. He's been there for many years. He read to you and taught you to play chess when your mother took you to visit him every week in the asylum. There was no loving home, Alice. There was no sailboat."

Alekhine had been listening, and he drew on Carroll again. *It's a poor sort of memory that only works backward. Look ahead, Alice, what do you remember?*

I suddenly remembered that there had indeed been a sailboat, I saw it in my memory, but it wasn't a real boat. It was an ugly painting of a sailboat in the corridor outside my father's hospital room. I heard my child's voice, talking to my father: "There's a painting of a boat in the hall."

My father: "Describe it to me."

It was hideous, but I made it picturesque. "It's golden and it has cinnamon sails and it's bound for Tahiti. It's heavy, loaded with spices and oranges, riding low in the water. No, wait, it changed. Now it's white and the sails are silver, filled with air. It carries diamonds and emeralds. The waves are splashing over the bow and throwing foam on the deck. The white queen is standing at the railing. Her face is wet and she's laughing."

Every day brought a different reality, a new world, for my father, and now, for me. New and confusing and violent and beautiful.

I fingered the red welt on my cheek. From the doorway, Jack said, "Your doctor called. He wants me to commit you tomorrow for another round of shock treatments."

I couldn't listen. I put my hands over my ears that weren't there. My father was a prisoner, held in a black castle. I remembered how he'd handed the castle piece to me.

"The castle lurks in a dark corner, tolerating no variation, and moves only in a straight line, crushing everything in its way. Some people call it a rook. Isn't that an ugly word?"

I ignored Jack and climbed into my bed and pulled the covers over my head, just as I had when I was a child. Alekhine came with me and whispered all night.

THE NEXT MORNING, I had completely vanished. Vampire reflection. I fumbled into my clothes, putting them on a body I couldn't see. I sat on the porch swing and watched Jack leave. He said, "I'm going to the convention, but I'll be home early. Pack for the hospital. I'll admit you this evening."

I glanced down at my shoes resting on the floor, the inside a bit scuffed and faded from the friction of my sole. I watched Jack drive away. Suddenly I heard voices in the flowerbed. They were hissing for my attention. Curious, the toad lilies and monkey grass had never made a sound, not even when I covered them with manure. A familiar voice rose out of the whispers.

The white queen can move in any direction, any direction, Alice. She can attack from across the board, she can live, live, live in reverse. Attack is the best defense.

"Alekhine?"

A pawn doesn't attack head-on, no, no, but to the side. It seems insignificant, overlooked, and this gives it the advantage of surprise. Surprise, Alice, big surprise. Open your eyes, Alice. Surprise! Four eyes, Alice. Four moves! Attack! Attack!

"I don't know how to attack."

Think large, Alice Smiley, think gigantic. Imagine more, dive deeper. Be outrageous, unprecedented. Be blind and see!

Alekhine's opponents had feared him because he had no need for sight to design a reality. Even blindfolded, he saw more than anyone else. He'd seen the best path for each chess piece, on 1,708 squares, in 28 games, all in his head.

Lewis Carroll told you to believe six impossible things before breakfast! He said if you don't know where you're going, any road will get you there!

I closed my eyes and it all became clear. I saw my road to escape in four moves.

FOR MY FIRST move, I went to the bank and took half the balances in our checking and savings accounts. Luckily, even when I became symptomatic, Jack never bothered to take me off the accounts. He didn't want to explain to the bank that his wife wasn't competent, so he simply locked away the checkbook and passbook, but I knew where he kept them.

The teller said, "Certainly Mrs. Smiley, right away."

She gave me stacks of hundred dollar bills and a few twenties for the long trip. I was on the offense, using a pawn's sideways attack, but offense is always better than defense. I could be any piece in the game, or all of them, and if I hurried, I just might make it across the board before Jack came home and found that he'd underestimated me.

For my second move, I loaded all of Jack's *Star Trek* collections into trash bags and drove to the nearest charity collection box and threw them in. Children I'd never meet would build safe new worlds of imagination with them. Besides, I thought Jack would waste much more time to trying to locate his toys then trying to locate me.

I went home and packed and took a cab to the airport. I sat in the waiting area, jiggling my knees, ready to go. A man stood across from me, watching. He was a cop in uniform, but he may have been one of the Village People. There was no way to tell, so I looked away quickly. He said, "Hello, ma'am, nervous about flying?"

I said, "I don't like to fly, I like to sail." I began humming YMCA to see if he'd break into a dance, making the letters with his arms, but he simply strolled away.

I ate an airport burger and fries from a paper bag. Nobody told me I had to finish it. A few minutes later I heard the call for my row. I put my cell phone in the bag with the remnants of my lunch and pitched it in the trash.

For my third move, I hurried down the boarding tunnel. I felt as though I might come out of the tunnel reinvented, ready to step inside the big silver Mylar plane. The words on the plane might say "Bon Voyage" or "Congratulations," they both applied. I'd soon become a tiny dot against a sky so bright it would've made Jack's eyes water to watch it. I'd flash like a crystal in the sun, jets roaring, helium swelling and exploding in the thin atmosphere, coming down fast to any place that wasn't here and now. The flight attendant stood at the door of the plane like a sentry at a gate. There was an air of solid defense about her and I knew she was a pawn. She saw my wild eyes, zoo eyes, and she said, "Hello, welcome aboard."

Alekhine whispered in my ear. *The pawn guards the gate. The white queen can go where she pleases.*

I buckled into my seat and wrapped myself in the grace of roaring engines as the plane rose and leveled off while I breathed cool, silver air. I looked out the window through the growing dusk at the square grid of fields below. I was living in reverse now, literally gaining time by flying west, going home to Tulsa at last. The earth was far below, turning in the opposite direction and taking Jack with it, riding on a disordered crust of rocks and manure with the chaos of his raided bank accounts and missing toys.

I sat quietly, wondering what my forth move would be. Evening fell and it grew dark outside the plane's small window. Suddenly, there was Alekhine's voice, the last time I would ever hear him, but I didn't know it then. He had led me through my opening game, and Jack's end game, and Alekhine's game was done. *Time for the fourth move, Alice, the attainment of clarity. Look at the window, at the window, Alice.*

She's here.

I studied the window glass, letting my eyes slide out of focus. Suddenly there she was. I saw her face. Alekhine had been right; she was in the glass, a ghostly, transparent reflection looking back at me. The white queen was invisible no longer. She had my face. I smiled and she smiled because she hadn't gone far away after all. She'd only been out riding the borders and testing the boundaries of exile, until Alekhine led her to a break in the fence.

PERPETUAL REBOOT

"I like a bit of a mongrel myself,
whether it's a man or a dog.
They're the best for everyday."
~George Bernard Shaw

PSYCHOLOGISTS AND SEX experts tell us there's nothing wrong with pornography, in moderation. Moderate porn? Is there such a thing? They say porn has its place, but they think the place isn't high school. Anybody who buys that idea doesn't know crap about teenage boys. Raid the lockers and book bags if you dare, and tell me what you find. Yeah. I'm speaking from experience, here. I know the porn business better than most people. Porn's the reason I was temporarily the richest kid in St. Bernard High School.

For a few hours, I was flush.

The start of my empire sprouted from a homework assignment that went wrong before it went right, and then it went wrong again. I'm in photography class, right? And we're told to snap a quick succession of shots of an event in nature to make a flip book. If you flip through the pages real fast, the pictures seem to move. Other students snap butterflies flapping their wings or flowers swaying, but I get to the core of nature and photograph two dogs humping, which makes for terrific repetitive action, but it's a poor choice for homework, in the tight-assed teacher's opinion. The other guys in the class give me hearty thumbs-up behind his back.

I stand there like a hypocrite and agree with the teacher that my project is a little edgy, but the high fives and the affirmation from the other guys let me know that my work has a limited but enthusiastic audience. This lesson isn't lost on me, which shows that I'm capable of learning from my mistakes. I refuse to back down, and make a heartfelt argument that my project literally has an underbelly sort of merit, but the uptight knob of a teacher sends me to Principal Smiley's office anyway.

Principal Jack Smiley, the *Star Trek* junkie. What a pompous nerdy tool. I'm wishing for a hidden camera when Smiley thumbs through my flip book because his face turns purple and his neck veins pop out. Smiley hates me instantly and wants to crush me, but all he can do legally is phone my grandfather and send me to detention. I live with my gramps, and fortunately, the old guy has a hell of a sense of humor and a healthy, if creepy, appreciation of porn, so no problem there.

Next, Smiley banishes me to detention for three afternoons after school. He turns me over to the pervy janitor and soon I'm mopping the boy's showers while the janitor ogles a porn magazine in his workroom recliner. Talk about your flip book. The irony isn't lost on me.

Fortunately, inspiration springs from adversity. I discover that the boy's shower backs up to the girl's shower on the other side of the wall. Our school is hosting an Allied Community Colleges cheerleading competition the next weekend, and I've always been quick to recognize an opportunity. If destiny sits on my side of the field, come Saturday there'll be genuine grown-up college chicks, really hot, mature ones, naked and soapy, on the other side of this very wall.

On Saturday, I go back to school and blend into the college crowd gathered for cheerleading events. I pick the lock on the photo lab and borrow a camera and fetch a cordless drill from the janitor's shed to make a lens-sized peephole in the great shower wall of opportunity. Then I sit back and wait. Just about the time I'm starting to doubt the wisdom of my venture, cheerleaders come giggling in, and it's show time in the showers. The next day is Sunday, peaceful, quiet, the distraction of church and all that stuff, and a perfect opportunity for me to develop film and print pics in the school lab.

I've never been so thankful that I paid attention in class. The monotonous drone about F-stops and other tedious details of light and focus and developing fluids and crap is useful at last. Maybe it's the inspiration of the moment, but I'm amazed at the quality of the pictures I produce. I jump on my bike and head home with dynamite soapy nude shots of twenty year old college chicks, arty and impressive, if I say so myself. They're downright, ass-kicking stunners.

MONDAY MORNING FINDS me back at school in the senior parking lot, discretely selling Calgon moments like hotcakes. They practically sell themselves because I'm marketing college girls in their early twenties to their target audience, namely high school boys with acne and delusions of hope. When I see the enthusiasm, I'm just sorry I didn't have a movie camera so I could put those cheerleaders on the Internet. In the porn arena, movies are miles ahead of still shots.

I'm advancing my fortune and fueling adolescent dreams, which means everybody's a winner, except maybe the cheerleaders, but I didn't turn them into sex objects. They did that to themselves. I'm just documenting their status. The pics are selling as fast as I can hand them out, at two bucks a shot. My pockets are bulging with money when Smiley suddenly clamps his hand around the back of my neck.

I have to confess that I'm often guilty of the crime of "didn't think." I didn't think of selling my enterprise off campus, but adolescent boys are my target market, right? I believe in a workable sales plan. I think it demonstrates a level of promotional savvy. If you're marketing to high school boys, you actually have to be at a high school, where this sort of stuff sells.

Smiley confiscates my unsold photos and threatens to call the vice squad, but I know he won't do it. Those cheerleaders have daddies and daddies have lawyers who'll swoop down on the school like a flock of crows in suits. Smiley has me, but I have him too, so we arrive at a deal. He offers to forget my slip in judgment in return for all pics plus negatives, so I take the deal, hand them over, and go to class like it's just another boring day. Fortunately, he didn't ask for my profits. I think he would have, if he'd thought of it, but he seemed distracted by the photos.

Being flush with cash, I ride my bike to the quick mart that night and score a six-pack from the store and some weed in the parking lot. I kill the brews and a couple of joints and oversleep the next morning, so I'm late for class. Once again, it's a lesson in the dangers of "didn't think."

First bell has already rung and I'm bolting through empty halls when Smiley takes me down like a cheetah cutting off a diseased gazelle from the herd. I'm yanked into his office, frisked, and slammed into a chair. He says he wants to be sure I'm not bringing more "disgusting" pictures to school, so, he goes through my book bag and discovers my stash of weed. Yeah, I hid it in my book bag. What was I gonna do? Leave it at home for my gramps to find and smoke? Let him buy his own.

Smiley's grinning, literally grinning, as he picks up the phone and calls the cops because I've brought drugs on campus. I'll admit I totally panic, so I dash into Smiley's personal toilet. I lock myself in his middle management shitter and curl up on the floor, shaking like a Chihuahua. From my lowered eyeshot, I spot the edge of a manila envelope hidden under the bathroom radiator. I pull it out and discover a few of my cheerleader pics, the really nasty ones, lots of soapy tits and foamy bush.

Of course, I'm jolted, but in a good way. Don't you love it when that happens? I shove a choice pic under the door to show Smiley that I've found his nasty bathroom stash, and he screams like a girl and tries to tear the door down. I taunt him verbally because I know it's too late for him to cancel the cops. I tell Smiley that I plan to show them exactly how our principal spends his bathroom breaks.

Cops show up and I hear Smiley outside the door, trying to send them away, but they tell him dope's a crime and it's out of his hands. A cop negotiator begins cooing my name through the door with projectile empathy: *Butch, Buuutch.* It appears they plan to play it soft because a news van with a satellite dish on top has just pulled into the parking lot.

Meanwhile, cops evacuate the whole school, creating mindless chaos in the halls and setting off alarms. I peek out the window and see a sniper with a night scope, just in case there's a drug cartel involved. The news team spots me at the window and all cameras swing my way. The sniper does too, taking aim. I drop to the floor.

Above my head, window glass suddenly breaks as a canister of tear gas hits the floor. I'm covered in glass and gasping in a choking cloud that fills the room, so I'm forced to open the door and step into the waiting arms of the law while Smiley dashes past me into the toxic cloud to grab the envelope, but he's in for a surprise. It's empty. I've stashed the pics in my boots. Smiley shakes the envelope and hacks tear gas and glares at me with red, streaming eyes.

"See ya downtown," I say as I flip him off before they cuff me.

I realize a drug bust will go badly for me because of my age. By the time I work through the courts, I'll turn eighteen and I'll be sent to the big boy prison where guys like me get reamed six ways from the south end. Cops are about to lead me away when Smiley tells them to wait a minute, he's sure he's made a mistake, it wasn't pot after all, just probably snuff, all the boys use it.

It's a fad, ha-ha. So sorry, his mistake.

Cops assure him that it certainly was pot, they checked it out, but when they try to show him the evidence bag, it has mysteriously disappeared from the open evidence kit left unguarded in Smiley's presence. Without the pot, they're forced to uncuff me and let me go. Smiley hustles the cops out of his office and shuts the door. He turns to face me and sticks out his hand. I fish the pics from my boot and hand them over. Live long and prosper, you *Star Trek* jackass. Then I go home to rest. What a morning.

Next day, I cruise back to school, but shithead Smiley blocks me at the door with expulsion papers. I'm tossed out like a bad school lunch. No decent school will have me now, not even the Catholics, who rush to judgment, in my opinion, seeing as how they're religious and all. I refuse to go to the alternate school for reprobates. I'm not one of those losers, all evidence to the contrary. I'm a businessman.

AT HOME, I kick back and watch daytime TV for a couple of weeks to recuperate, which gramps mistakes for lying around the house, so he says I have to go out and prove myself. He says I should find a job to help me reboot my life. He's so precious when he tries to talk like modern people. He's not so adorable, though, when he says he'll kick me out of the house if I don't do what he says.

He makes a few calls to friends to find a job for me. He hangs up the phone and suggests I talk to his buddies Clarence the Dwarf and Rudy the Hunchback because they run a business and need an apprentice. Gramps tells me to hurry over, Clarence the Dwarf wants to meet me. I go under protest, but it takes a while to get there on my bike, mostly because I lift a six-pack to prop up my nerves. Finally, I arrive with sullen eyes and Coors breath.

I straddle my bike and squint up at the name on the front of the building.

Perpetual Remembrance Monuments

I can't believe Gramps found me a job in a frigging spooky tombstone factory. I think Oh no, I've been here before, but not in daylight. I have an unfortunate history of minor midnight vandalism at this location because it just screams for defacement. Out front they display blank headstones that can be seen from the street. Me and my buddies occasionally sneak over on Saturday nights and spray paint the blank headstones with obscenities for the benefit of the congregation going into the Holiness Church across the street on Sunday mornings.

I work up the nerve to drag myself through the front door, thankful that I was never caught on camera, ratted on, or otherwise implicated. It could make for a very uncomfortable job interview. This place brings to mind a dozen low-budget horror movies where cocky teenage guys with hot girlfriends are captured by hooded ghouls, chained to rusty plumbing, and subjected to chain saws.

As gramps said, there are two mutants inside the building. First, I see, and hear, a tall hunchback named Rudy, yelling into a phone. Rudy's an impressive verbal sniper with a cool British accent.

"Cretinous lout!" he screams. "You idiotic whore mongering clod!"

I've never heard such classy obscenities. It's like James Bond really lost his temper. Maybe the hunchback is out of sorts because of his deformity. Talk about a perpetual chip on your shoulder. This guy's chip comes standard.

Next, I see a sweet-faced dwarf sitting at an engraving table, cutting letters into a slab of marble. This must be Clarence. In his little

Yoda hand he grips a water-cooled drill. His stubby feet hang off the edge of the chair. His eyes have a look of patience and understanding through his stone cutter goggles.

Rudy hangs up and walks over to Clarence and says, "The obtuse shipping clerk misdirected the stones. The lot's delayed until next week and the defrauder won't make good on the shipping."

Clarence stops drilling and looks up. "Maybe they'd be a little more flexible if you'd stop calling them names they can't understand."

With this, the mutants launch into a loud argument. Above the shouting, a high pitched voice belts "Dunka-shane" out of an old radio. The dial's set on WIRA ("Golden oldies for all you olden goldies"), dinosaur music with saccharine lyrics about love and hope, interspersed with ads for laxatives and retirement fund counseling, on-line dating for senior citizens, and burial plot advice. As I look around, the announcer tells me that I can now have my diabetes medicine delivered directly to my door.

The argument escalates and Clarence lobs a chunk of granite in Rudy's direction. It hits the wall next to my head and that's when they notice me standing by the door. The announcer says that my claim cannot be denied for any reason as the two of them stroll over and begin to conduct a job interview.

This is me and the dwarf:
"Who are you?"
"Butch, your new employee."
"What's your real name?"
"It sucks. I'd rather not say. "
"Why are you here?"
"To talk about the job."
"What makes you think there's a job?"
"My gramps said so."

Clarence grins. "Actually you're right, there's a job. We need a really strong boy to move slabs of marble and granite with a block and tackle. Four, five hundred pound slabs. You move them to the carving bench where I inscribe them. After that, they're driven to the cemetery and put into place with a crane."

"Can't drive. They took away my license."

Clarence stops grinning. "Why?"

"Some little misunderstanding about leaving the scene, I can't remember exactly because I was a little over the legal limit, so it would've been irresponsible of me to stick around for a sobriety test."

In his helium voice, Clarence says, "Tell me about your criminal record and don't leave anything out."

The more I tell him, the more he grins. "You're not so bad," he says.

I believe short people are unreasonably optimistic. Maybe things don't look as hopeless from down there.

The mutants go into a huddle while I slouch. On the radio, Little Richard yells out for his tootie frootie. I'm listening to an ad for Carnival's geriatric cruise on the Varicose Princess when they call me over. Rudy the Hunchback does the talking this time.

"You're obviously clever, or you'd be incarcerated. You're a common criminal, but there's nothing here you can steal. If you don't find gainful employment, your grandfather will kick you out, so we can underpay you and overwork you and you can't resign. Your grandfather wants you rebooted, so to speak, or so he says. Well, welcome to the Perpetual Monuments perpetual reboot camp, my good fellow. You're about to enter a strange world of human metamorphosis, dear boy, because we're going to turn you into a new entity."

Oh damn, they're giving me the job, at least I think they are, if I've got the translation right. Obviously my bad attitude didn't work its magic, but given time, I can disgust almost everybody, especially classy people. I'll be out of here in no time. It's Friday afternoon, so they tell me to report to work Monday morning, bright and early. A Dean Martin song follows me out the door describing how love is like a pizza pie that hits you in the eye.

That night I get totally trashed, stagger to Principal Smiley's house at midnight, and spell out DICKHEAD on his perfect lawn with grass killer, along with a large corresponding illustration, the best one I can manage, using a spray can of Grass Blast.

Monday morning, I'm an hour late to work. When I get there, I lounge, riding the minimum wage pony, combing my hair and chain-smoking with indifference. Finally, Rudy orders me to go out front and clean up the entrance, mow the grass, pick up trash, and clean Saturday night's graffiti off the headstones.

I fool around out front and lob pieces of trash into the street and weed-eat the grass until it looks like a bad haircut. Next, I squat in front of the stones and scrub off the obscenities with paint thinner in big loopy smears, hoping all the while that dudes from my school won't drive by and heap ridicule. I surprise myself by actually missing the old gang. In days gone by, we'd snort pilfered Adderall from the school nurse's office (major buzz with undercurrents of invincibility), and then we'd paint these headstones. I never thought I'd be cleaning them off.

It appears that I've fallen, accidentally, into some kind of sentimental soup. My stomach gets weird, empty, like I'd thrown up. I ooze schmaltz about my lost youth, or maybe I've just breathed too much paint thinner. I finish and go inside, sweating, covered with grass clippings, and reeking of acetone. It's Elvis week on WIRA and he's belting out a song about how everybody on the old cell block is dancing. Yeah, right, I know about that place. Nobody's dancing, believe me. What appears to be dancing is actually ducking and dodging.

"Set up the block and tackle, my good fellow!" Clarence barks and slaps me on the back. "We've got some marble to move."

I look at a zillion marble slabs, each weighing several hundred pounds, stacked like dominoes. For hours, I sort them according to size and color and any other damn classification Rudy comes up with. He hangs over my shoulder, giving orders in my ear and pointing. I quickly discover that faked incompetence is not a safe approach when using a block and tackle, so I carefully move the bitching things, tons of them, until my back screams and my legs are in knots and my palms are covered with rope blisters. A silky radio announcer tells me that part of my medical expenses might be covered by Medicare.

By six o'clock I'm so beat I can barely stagger out the door. The radio advises me to ask my doctor if a free sample of Viagra is right for me.

Clarence says, "See you tomorrow." Then he adds, "You did a

good job today, Butch."

"Uhh . . . thanks," I mutter.

Overhead, Elvis growls and grumbles.

I'm too wiped out to ride my bike home, so I slowly roll it as I limp through the twilight streets. Gramps has supper ready, I thank him, but I'm not able to eat because I hurt all over. I fall across my bed, fully dressed.

I thank my mattress for being soft.

I bless my blanket and my pillow.

DAYS PASS. THEY just pass, that's all. Leave it alone. I hoist tons of marble with the block and tackle. Every morning, Rudy wants the piles rearranged. My blisters tear open and leak. In spite of myself, I'm learning the words to codger tunes. I develop symptoms in the health commercials. I'm convinced that my cholesterol is dangerously high. I suffer from urinary frequency. My joints ache. Constipation and glaucoma are looming possibilities. I fret that my insufficient retirement investments won't see me through my golden years. Overhead, some guy sings about the Copa-ca-baaa-na. Slick ads push Ex-Lax, Claritin, Zocor.

This is the first time in my life that I can't pull an option out of thin air. I have to hold down this job or get kicked out of the house and I can't live on the streets because, with my record, I'd end up in jail. This job's preferable to jail only in the fact that Rudy and Clarence aren't planning to cornhole me on a daily basis, not in the usual sense. Meanwhile, my old gang carries on without me, bashing nerds, drag racing down Main Street, and lying about getting laid. I scrub their graffiti off the headstones. My fingers peel from paint thinner.

I hear Rudy on the phone, shouting at European marble suppliers. Foreign guys who tear marble out of the earth must be tough, but they don't scare Rudy. He yells at them in Italian or French, spewing exotic obscenities and making threats, until the slabs roll into town on a train car. When they arrive, Rudy and I drive to the freight yard to pick them up. I hate riding with him because his hump forces him to practically lie on the steering wheel. Even worse, I can feel his judgment of me like a third passenger in the truck. It fills the air and crawls on my skin like ants. I wish I had some trick to make him approve of me.

Then one day, in the truck, it just happens. All it took was three words. I look out the car window and softly say, "Marble's beautiful . . . totally."

Rudy's quiet for a block or two, then he starts to talk. He fills the truck with his classy accent. He describes marble's transparency; how it grabs light, changes it, and sends it out again. Translucent, he calls it. He doesn't use his rough telephone voice. It's hard to believe that somebody so ugly can sound so elegant. He could be an actor on an old radio show, making the ladies swoon, until they saw his hideous deformity, and then they'd look away in disgust. I know it and he knows it. His life is in his voice and when he speaks, his words are bubbles, rising full of air and light, not anchored by his twisted spine. He says, "Butch, if you polish marble, you can look into the heart of the stone. Veins run through marble, just as they run through human tissue. It's quite astounding."

He talks about marble all the way to the freight yard, and while we're loading, and while we're driving back. He tells me grain, he tells me veins, he tells me color and clarity. At the shop, we unload the slabs and he slides his hands over the stone's flawless face. He's full of reverence for nature's perfection and his own face, in that moment, is not nearly so hideous.

Clarence walks up behind me and asks, "What's with him?"

I answer, "He talked . . . totally."

Clarence laughs, as though what I said was funny. "Butch, you're a stone groove." The little dwarf loves his job. Some people never get that lucky. When I watch him chuckling over some silliness on the radio, I wonder how he can have such an imperfect body and yet be so perfectly happy.

Some things look better from a distance, and some things look better up close. From a distance, Clarence's headstones are lumps of rock, but nearer, you see the words cut into the stone, precise and dependable, and what they say, and what they mean. Everything has its own flattering distance. Clarence just looks better up close. Most small things do.

SUDDENLY AND WITHOUT warning, the mutants have a terrible argument, worse than all the others. I can't figure it out because they talk in code. They've been together so long they're like married people, with a life and a language that's private. The argument doesn't mellow or fade.

Rudy stews for days, storing resentment in his hump the way camels store water. The two of them don't speak, but the radio fills up the sound holes. Rudy and I play cards, listening to Barry Manilow Live! and John Denver dead, but still thanking God he's a country boy. We heat up tomato soup in the microwave. I watch Rudy build a house of cards that collapses without warning. We buy scratch lottery tickets and even win a few bucks. We wait for something to happen.

At last, Clarence shuffles up to the table where we're playing rummy. He says, "Rudy, I thought about it and you were right all along—totally, as Butch says."

Rudy acts surprised, but then he laughs. The argument is over, just like that. I can tell because the air changes.

Later, I tell Clarence, "That was nice, what you did, letting Rudy win."

He says, "Being right is more important to him than it is to me. Being right is all some people have."

I know what he means. Being a punk is all some people have, too.

I WORK THROUGHOUT the rest of the school year while my classmates graduate from good old St. Bernard High. I'm miserable with jealousy because they finished school and I didn't, but I have to admit I got an education too. I worked; hard work that would make most of them fold like Rudy's house of cards. I earned every blister, every ache and pain. I learned what I could do, and I learned that it was more than I believed I could do, even while I was doing it.

I thought marble was something to spray-paint with obscenities. I never looked at it before and admired its age and its adaptability, it's willingness to be carved and cut and transformed. I watched Clarence cutting precise images into the marble and I realized that an artist absorbs beauty through his eyes and ears and sends it out through his hands, enriched by everything that artist knows and believes.

Grandpa says he's proud of me for sticking with a difficult job. He tells me to quit my job and enjoy the summer with my friends. The praise and the idea of freedom make me starry-eyed. I tell Rudy and Clarence I'm quitting so I can spend the summer learning to be a kid again. They wish me well and even hug me before I split. Splitting isn't as easy as I thought it would be.

During the summer, I drop by to talk to Rudy and Clarence. I tell them I'm a good photographer and want to study cinematography in college and maybe get a job in TV or movies, so I guess it's a GED for me because every decent high school in town has turned me down.

Then, just like in the movies, a miracle happens.

A few days before the new school year starts, Rudy and Clarence pay a call on Principal Smiley and firmly suggest that he take me back. Smiley balks, but under the weight of high octane mutant pressure, he folds. Smiley says I can come back if I make concessions. I have to cut my hair, tuck in my shirt, and pull up my pants. He even suggests a pocket protector. I can't be Butch anymore. Butch is a remnant of my past. I have to use my real name, which is—don't laugh—Elmer, as in Elmer Fudd, and if you make fun, I'll kill you while you sleep. In other words, I have to nerd-up. Oh, well, the world's richest men are nerds. Nerd is the new cool.

There's a photo on the wall next to my bed. I look at it every night before I go to sleep. In the picture, I'm standing in front of the monument shop with Rudy on one side of me and Clarence on the other. The sign *Perpetual Remembrance Monuments* is behind us, above our heads. I've got one hand stretched down, resting on Clarence's shoulder. My other arm is draped around Rudy's hump.

Rudy and Clarence are giving the camera a thumbs-up. The picture looks out of place among all the soapy cheerleaders on my wall, but punk or lawful, deformed or straight, everything has a place.

Dunka-Shane.

FLIGHT PATH

"If you pick up a starving dog and make him
prosperous, he will not bite you. That is the
principal difference between a dog and a man."
~Mark Twain

HERE ON THE coast, old timers tell of tiny silver fish that fall from the sky with the afternoon rain. It's not science fiction; it simply means that air currents can lift anything. The moist wind scoops up little fish from the Gulf along with small green leaves of marine vegetation and gelatinous eggs of sea creatures. These rich organic clouds drift onto the coast and dissolve into rain. The downpour of marine life hits hot rooftops and sidewalks where it sizzles and vaporizes into powdery steam, leaving nothing but a flaking salty parchment on the pavement. As it dries, an exotic vapor rises, carrying the heady smell of the Amazon or the far southern origins of the Nile. After such rains, the lavender and gold sunsets are a photographer's dream. I should know, I once made my living taking pretty pictures.

I'm not a stupid man, just gullible. I knew that the wind could move unlikely things; I just didn't understand the aerodynamics of flight paths. Nobody told me that planes take off into the warm southern winds of summer and into the cold north winds in winter to benefit from the lift of a headwind. The scientific principle that lifts fish from the Gulf also elevates tons of steel and baggage and human cargo. I've learned all this now, when it's too late to save everything I ever cared about, and what I cared about most was my wife, Marilyn.

I can't tell you why Marilyn put up with me; I was never a prize. I had the pallor of one who spent his days in eerie safe-lit developing rooms with trays of pungent darkroom liquids. She learned to tolerate the smell of chemicals on my hands. We led the life of gypsies. Too often, my teaching grants ran out and Marilyn was required to pack up, tell old neighbors goodbye, and smile her way through the glad-handing of a new faculty in some replacement job I'd found. Her life was a succession of adjustments and acclimations. At last she asked if we could go home and settle down, and I agreed. I would've done anything to please Marilyn. She was so lovely, and I marveled that she married the likes of me, a basset hound of a guy, dumpy, unremarkable, except for my perceptiveness with viewfinders. One look at my wife and you'd realize I had an eye for beauty.

I brought Marilyn home to St. Bernard Parrish as she asked, but I had very few job options. I finally landed a position as photography teacher at St. Bernard High School, although I was vastly overqualified and the pay was pitiful. My new job started after the Christmas break, which meant that we had to find a new home fast. That's how we came to be standing with a real estate agent in a Swiss-style housing development on a cold December day.

All married couples have their small moments of pending tragedy, those sharp-edged turning points where, if either of them had noticed their position on the tip of the blade, they could've jumped clear, hand in hand, and landed on their feet. Our greatest shame, Marilyn's and mine, was that there was nothing in our wonderful mental synergy that could've predicted this tragedy disguised as a blessing.

So here we were, touring a charming community recently built on the outskirts of town, near the southern end of the local airport. A dozen alpine cottages hugged a horseshoe street, ever so much the architecture of Heidi, but on a flat pasture instead of in the Alps. Attention was given to the exterior details: peaked gables, gingerbread trim, arched doorways, and creamy stucco. A landscaper had installed cobblestone sidewalks and lantern streetlights.

"Oh Bill, it's so sweet and charming," Marilyn whispered.

We shared a cautious optimism and we took hands subtly, so the realtor couldn't see. In that clasp of fingers was an unspoken agreement to buy this pretty little house, a Swiss cottage out of my dreams. I've always had a yen for the Alps, although I've never actually stood on top of a mountain. I wanted to go climbing with a camera slung on my neck, capturing images of snowy peaks and valleys. Marilyn, bless her, just wanted a permanent home.

We completed our tour of the interior and stood on the new sod of the front yard of the last available house for sale; a cheery little home that seemed to emit an aura of permanence. A winter wind gusted around our ears and squares of dead grass as lifeless as failed skin grafts spread brown and dormant below our feet.

"It's perfect," said Marilyn, "but it's awfully near the airport. What about the noise of planes? Will it be a problem?"

Just then, as if on assignment from the realtor, a descending plane passed overhead, heading north into the wind to bank for a landing on the far side of the airport. It glided almost silently, only a whisper splitting the air as its shadow zipped over the front yard.

"You see, there's hardly any sound," the real estate agent said. "You won't even hear it when you're inside, and barely hear it outside. It's really no problem at all."

"See?" I echoed, "No problem at all. And this is the last house for sale in the neighborhood."

I was so charmed by the alpine setting that I could almost hear yodeling. I moved forward and stepped up, trance-like, onto the porch and watched my ghostly image in the window inset of the front door. The pane of glass reflected my paunch and tuft of hair that lifted in the wind. There seemed to be two of me, one on the inside peering out, watching as the second me approached. I reached with my stained fingers and touched the glass and my ghostly reflection reached back, brushing fingertips. From the brown lawn, the agent watched me and asked Marilyn, "How long have you and Bill been married?"

"Fourteen years," answered Marilyn, "but we were childhood sweethearts. We've known each other all our lives."

"No children?" asked the realtor.

Marilyn gave her stock answer. "Not yet."

Our lives together had been too lateral for the ups and downs of raising children. It was always something we intended to do later, until parenthood eventually became like a figure in one of my photographs. It was a concept from a former time.

"Nice to be married to someone you know so well," the agent said.

Marilyn smiled. "Yes. We've never even had a real argument."

I didn't participate in the conversation. I was too busy gazing through the glass with the flat of my hand shielding my eyes. Just then, another plane whispered overhead. "Hardly any noise at all," I said softly.

We were innocent, uninitiated. We didn't know that airplane landings, being controlled falls, are typically quiet. The plane's nose is pointed down, engines pointed up and barely purring, no thrust as the plane sinks slowly on a cushion of air. Moreover, it was December, so all takes offs and departures were on the north end of the runway, far from the cottages of St. Bernard Acres.

We returned to Marilyn's mother's house to do the math. I was animated, pacing. "If we act now, we can move in by Christmas. We'll unpack and settle down before the semester starts. I really love that house!"

Sitting cross-legged on the bed, Marilyn leaned over a notebook and ran her finger down a balance sheet. "It's a stretch, but we can barely afford it as long as things go smoothly. But it's a new house, what can happen?" I grinned at my stunning wife. That may well have been the moment of my most perfect love for her.

I phoned our realtor that night and made an offer that was accepted without a quibble. The day we signed loan papers and took possession of new keys was one of the happiest in my memory. We gave the moving company our new address and the occasion seemed to be more than a simple continuation of our days together. It was such a clean start that I thought we might at last begin a family in that house.

AFTER CHRISTMAS, WE settled into a contented routine. I passed my days at work in the classroom and darkroom. Elmer, a pocket-protected student in the senior class, came around and asked to be my photo lab assistant. I liked the boy's enthusiasm. He seemed more mature than the rest of the students and rather nerdy like me, so I took him on.

At home, Marilyn unpacked boxes and prepared our evening meals. We took coffee together at a table in the garden, when the air was warm enough. Over our coffee, I recited the hours of my day and Marilyn showed me swatches and paint chips, laying the samples on the table between us. Sometimes the purr of a plane passed overhead, a crucifix-shaped shadow that slid almost silently over the table. Throughout the night, cargo planes continued to depart and land, using the runway to the north, but we never heard them. "I love this house," I said one morning as I stood in the center of our lovely living room.

"Yes Bill, everything's perfect," she answered as she positioned a vase of artificial flowers on the new coffee table.

"Except for one detail," I added.

Our harmony of thought was as finely tuned as ever. She nodded and said, "I think we'll plan that project for next year."

I smiled and pictured the two of us pushing a carriage on the horseshoe sidewalk of St. Bernard Acres, greeted by our admiring neighbors.

"In the meantime, let's get a dog," she suggested.

That afternoon, we went into town and adopted a puppy, a nervous little female Chihuahua. We named her Trixie. We had a delightful house and a cute pet and the support of each other and a stable future. We were living an American dream.

SPRING CAME, AND the cold winds of winter were replaced by warm winds from the Gulf to the south. Unknown to Marilyn and me, the airport authorities made their seasonal adjustment of flight paths. On the first night of the new trajectories, we'd been asleep for an hour when a horrible roar and vibration shook us awake. It was as though a train had zoomed through the bedroom.

"My God!" I screamed, sitting up in bed.

"What is it? What is it?" Marilyn cried, clinging to me.

Trixie jumped on the bed and tunneled under the covers, shaking. Then, just as quickly as it had come, the horrible roar was gone, leaving behind only a numbing echo in our ears. "It was a plane." I said as I went to the window and looked into the starry sky. "It had to be. But so loud! And at eleven at night?"

"I'll go to the airport tomorrow and ask them about it," Marilyn said from the bed. "It must've been off course. I thought it was going to crash into us."

We went back to sleep, but at four in the morning, the brutal scenario was repeated: the roaring, vibrating, clutching, screaming, Trixie barking frantically. Bleary-eyed and exhausted, I went to work and Marilyn drove the short distance to the Airport Authorities. She was directed to the Noise Abatement Office to speak with an official, the peculiar Mr. Box.

"Oh, yes," Box told her, "Eleven and four, that would be correct." He was a short boxy man, as square-cornered as his name. He wore his brown suit and tie as though he'd been born in them. Marilyn rubbed at the headache behind her temples.

She asked, "But what was it? We've never heard such horrible noises."

Box explained, "Freight planes, you know—cargo. Got to keep that merchandise rolling. They depart late at night and land early in the morning, best time to move freight. DC 8's usually, four-engine jobs. They have schedules to keep, moving all that stuff people buy on E-Bay and the Home Shopping Network." He smiled at his own wit. "There's the parcel delivery service and the U.S. mail, too, zooming over our heads. It all requires those big planes. And there'll be regular passenger flights, too, every day. Really loud, aren't they?"

Marilyn dropped her hands into her lap and squinted against the cheerful sunlight beaming through the window behind Box's desk. The corona of light formed a halo that gave him a saint-like innocence. "Yes, a horrible noise," she agreed, "but why now? We've never heard them before."

He shrugged. "It's time for the seasonal change, flight paths, you know. Started at eleven last night. Summer is the season of the winds from the south. It's all very technical." He squinted at Marilyn as though he were appraising her ability to understand the mechanics of flight.

Marilyn was incredulous. "You mean that noise is going to go on all summer?"

"Oh yes, for as long as the wind blows from the south. Didn't your real estate agent explain that to you?"

Marilyn left the airport in shock. She got out of our car in the driveway and knocked at the house next door. Mrs. Finch, a stooped widow with bilateral hearing aids, shuffled to the door in pompom slippers. "Oh, hello, Marilyn dear."

Marilyn burst into tears on the stoop.

"My goodness! Come in. Whatever's wrong?" Mrs. Finch guided her inside.

"It's the terrible noise!" Marilyn wailed. "Mrs. Finch, what will we do?"

The old lady looked past Marilyn, through her lacy curtains at the quiet street outside. "What noise, dear?"

"The planes! The planes! Didn't you hear them last night?"

Mrs. Finch waved a dismissive, veined hand. "Oh my dear, I take out my hearing aids when I go to bed. I'm so deaf I couldn't hear Gabriel blow his horn, but I did feel the house tremble a couple of times. I thought it was earthquakes. You say it was planes overhead? Well, that's a relief. I'd hate to see us all disappear into a fault line."

Marilyn dropped into a chintz chair overlaid by protective doilies. "Don't you understand? It's going to go on all summer, until the wind changes. Everything's been moved to the south runways. Eeeeek!"

Marilyn grabbed her ears as a passenger plane with three howling McDonald Douglas MD11 engines (known affectionately as Mad Dogs) skimmed over the rooftop, transporting three hundred conventioneers and their luggage to fun-filled Miami Beach.

Mrs. Finch jerked out both hearing aids and sighed with relief.

Marilyn gave up and went home to check on Trixie. When I came home that afternoon, she gave me the tragic news as she sobbed pitifully against my shoulder. I patted her hair.

"There, there. Maybe we'll get used to it."

She pulled back and glared. "Used to it, Bill? *Used to it?* We'll end up as deaf as Mrs. Finch!"

"There's no need for sarcasm," I pouted. "I didn't lay out the flight paths or decide on the direction of the wind."

"Go to the airport and talk to them," Marilyn begged. "You've got to convince them to stop. I can't do it; those chauvinists won't listen to a woman. This is inhuman, Bill, and maybe even illegal, I don't know. Even Trixie's a nervous wreck. She won't come out of the broom closet. Oh, our beautiful home!"

Given the historic track record of the average Joe's success in changing the course of governmental decrees I've always made a point of avoiding confrontation with authority figures, especially bureaucratic ones. It's foolish to put faith in the promises of politicians, as we all know. I gave Marilyn a placating smile. "Perhaps there'll only be a few planes, and not every day. Maybe it won't be so bad."

Just then, in mocking contradiction, a huge plane screamed overhead. Sadly, I would soon come to recognize the sound of the Boeing 737 with unbelievably loud Pratt and Whitney engines. Marilyn ran sobbing into our bedroom and slammed the door. I followed her and pressed my forehead against the closed door with resignation. "I'll go tomorrow and talk to them, dearest. I love this house too. It will all work out, I promise."

The next day, I found a substitute teacher for my morning classes and made an early call on Mr. Box at the Noise Abatement Office. Being awake half the night had given me time to reassess my aversion to conflict, and I'd developed a lush paranoia fueled by exhaustion and a strapping suspicion of authority. I refused the proffered chair and stood looming in front of his desk.

"Come clean, Box," I barked, "what's the plan?"

"Plan?" he echoed, blinking innocently.

With the conviction of a Midwestern sheepherder, I dramatically added, "Are you people trying to run us off our land so you can get your hands it?"

"Why would we want your . . . land?"

"For airport expansion, of course!"

He stuck out his chin. "See here! If the Airport Authority wanted your property, we'd simply take it. I'm afraid you're a victim of one of those land development scams by some unscrupulous contractor. They crop up around airports from time to time."

"A land development scam?" It seemed as though my paranoia had been justified.

Box lifted a stack of files from his desk and extended them toward me. "See this? The owners of eleven of the twelve houses in your neighborhood have filed complaints, including your wife. The only one I haven't heard from is a Mrs. Finch. She doesn't seem to mind the noise, or she might be dead in her house. I'd check if I were you."

My legs were suddenly undependable and I dropped into the chair he'd offered. "What about the contractor's scam? Get back to the scam!"

Box put down the files and flopped wearily into his own chair. "Oh yes. Well, you see, the way it works, a developer tosses up a community of cheaply built cracker box houses very near the end of a runway. Shoddy workmanship, poor materials. These houses were never meant to last. You must understand that they're going to fall down, especially when vibrated daily by jet engines. The developer makes the places look superficially good, gets inflated prices for them, and then bails with the money."

I was silent for a moment, trying to comprehend what Box had told me. "I don't understand. The developer could build shoddy houses anywhere. How does the airport figure into it?"

Box leaned across his desk on his forearms and spread his stubby fingers on his blotter. He whispered, "The NCP."

"NCP?"

"NCP—Noise Compatibility Program. You know, government funding to cover up the noise of planes. Didn't you hear what happened around the Atlanta airport when they expanded? The noise became intolerable to the neighbors, so the government went in and installed extra insulation, soundproof windows, central heat and air, things to cut down on the noise. They made the houses much better, and the owners didn't have to spend their own money on improvements. They call it noise abatement or mitigation, but it all adds up to the same thing. Repaired and improved houses."

I brightened. "You mean we could get these improvements to our house for free?"

Box shook his balding head. "Nope, afraid not. NCP money's gone now. Atlanta used it up."

"Then why are you telling me this, if there's no money?"

"Because now the government doesn't repair and improve houses any more. It simply buys them outright from a different fund. That fund's practically a bottomless pit of money."

I blinked in confusion. "You've lost me, Box."

Box grinned. "It's called an acquisition fund. These days, the government won't spend funds unless it acquires something. We recently spent 67 million for a massive home buy-out around the Charlotte airport and immediately leveled the houses into splinters. Nothing but vacant lots where 400 homes once stood. Same story all over the country. Who do you think owns all that empty land around airports? The federal government of course, by buying up shoddy development scams. As I said, pirate developers build cut-rate houses near airports, knowing that the government will have to buy them up and level them before very long."

I heard my voice go up an octave in disbelief. "Why doesn't the government just buy the land in the first place, before it's developed by these pirates?"

"Oh, that would never do. It would be purchasing. These funds aren't for purchasing, they're for acquiring."

"But it's only a matter of terminology!"

Box shrugged. "Everything the government does is terminology."

He opened a desk drawer and took out an antacid mint and popped it into his mouth. "Look, it's not what something is; it's what it's *called*. These situations work in the homeowner's favor because newspapers love this kind of story. The public doesn't care about shoddy workmanship, they only hear about planes shaking houses apart, so the government shells out dough to keeps things quiet. You might even get more than you paid, especially if you press for pain and suffering, that sort of thing. Everybody's happy, everybody wins. The developer never has to make good on his shoddy work, the homeowner sells a bad house for good money, and the government increases its land holdings in a valuable area."

"Valuable? How in God's name is the land valuable?"

"Because it's next to an airport, man, in case of runway expansion. Use your brain." Box helped himself to another antacid. "Take the government's money. Sell them your shoddy, crappy house. The feds won't mind. They're accustomed to paying ten grand for a toilet plunger."

"Shoddy? Crappy? I love my house, Box! Suppose I don't want

to sell?"

Box crunched the mint between his molars. "Take the money and buy something else. That house was never meant to last. You're sitting on a collapsing gold mine."

"We'll just see about that!"

I stormed out and went home to tell Marilyn. As I came through the front door, the doorknob fell off in my hand. I looked at it and dropped it into my coat pocket.

"Sell our house to the government?" Marilyn seemed intrigued.

"I can't believe you want to be a part of this scam!"

She shrugged. "Well, scam is a matter of viewpoint, don't you think?"

"I'll never sell!" I roared. "They think I'm powerless, but they're wrong. My whole life I've been pushed around by bullying bastards. Well, not anymore. I refuse to be bullied or acquired. I love this house!" I left to teach my afternoon classes.

AFTER WORK, I came home to find Marilyn in tears, curled at the end of the sofa, her knees drawn up. Trixie was cowering beside her. Marilyn pointed to the back yard with a soggy tissue in her hand. "Oh Bill, it rained a while ago. Now, there's something horrible out there. It fell with the rain." She sobbed harder.

I glanced out the window at the sunny afternoon. "Something horrible? Where?"

"On the ground!" She wailed, hiding her face in her hands.

I went out and saw white powdery streaks across the concrete apron, baking in the sun, as though strings of pale jelly had been flung there and left to dry. I couldn't make sense of it and certainly saw nothing to merit the fuss, but I changed my mind when I looked under the patio table and saw several slimy strings of pearls on the shady concrete, untouched by the sun. They appeared to be ribbons of fish eggs. I took a ballpoint pen from my shirt pocket and slid it under one of the draping strings, carefully lifted it, and brought it close to my face. Inside each egg I saw a tiny, thread-like whipping tail and the black pupil of a rudimentary eye looking back at me through cloudy yellow albumin. The eggs were identical all the way down the chain, like a repeating image in a fun-house mirror. I jumped at the sound of a voice behind me.

"They're jelly-fish eggs," said Mrs. Jenkins. She'd come out of her house to stand on the property line and gift me with an oceanographic tidbit. "They breed this time of year, so thick in the Gulf, you could walk across the top of them."

As she spoke, there was a loud squeal. She jerked both hearing aids out of her ears. "Oh these darn things! I think the airport puts out a sound wave that makes them act up." She bumped them against the heel of her hand.

I looked at the string of eggs draped across my pen. "I don't think they're jellyfish. Do jellyfish lay eggs and have eyes?"

There was no answer. When I glanced up, Mrs. Jenkins had gone indoors.

Marilyn watched me from the door, silently hugging herself. Trixie peeked from between Marilyn's ankles. I turned on the garden hose and washed the eggs across the property line into Mrs. Finch's yard, where they disappeared in the grass.

OVER THE NEXT few weeks, moving vans begin appearing in the neighborhood. By the end of April, everyone had been "acquired" except for Mrs. Finch and us. Box had evidently been working overtime.

"At least Mrs. Finch has integrity," I said, peeking through the drapes. "She won't sell out, either."

Marilyn and Trixie both glared at me with bleary, sleep-deprived eyes.

"Please sell," Marilyn pleaded, clinging to her box of Kleenex. "The terrible noise. I can't go on."

"Never! Never! I love this house!" I stamped my foot and heard the creak of an inadequate floor joist. A large piece of plaster fell from the ceiling, narrowly missing Trixie. Marilyn screamed when it hit the floor and flew apart. Trixie scratched desperately at the front door, so I let her out. Instead of doing her business in the grass as usual, the dog made a dash across the street and disappeared behind an abandoned house. We both ran after her, calling frantically, but she'd vanished. We covered the neighborhood on foot and finally cruised in the car, calling her name until we were hoarse. At midnight we gave up.

"Even the dog knows better than to stay here. I can't go on, I tell you," Marilyn muttered. Once again, she cried herself to sleep.

The next day, I walked the abandoned neighborhood, putting up useless "lost dog" signs. There was nobody left to read them. When I got home, I saw a moving van in front of Mrs. Finch's house.

"You see? Even Mrs. Finch knows when to leave," said Marilyn.

"She might have sold out, but I'll never be an acquisition," I declared.

Due to the stress, the loss of Trixie, my lack of sleep, I was beginning to fall apart at school. If it hadn't been for my lab assistant Elmer grading assignments and keeping the photo lab running, I would've been found out much earlier. Finally, my boss, Principal Jack Smiley, called me in. Encamped behind his barrier desk, he gestured toward a chair.

"Sit down, Bill . . . uh, do people call you Bill?"

"You can call me William," I snapped as I took a seat.

Smiley gave a "whatever" shrug and pressed on. "Bill, it has come to my attention that you haven't been making your classes." He tented his fingers, resting his chin on his manicured fingertips. He grinned at me.

I looked across the desk and knew I'd dealt with him before.

You, Smiley, I know you very well. You're the bully on the playground who pushes the little kids off the swings when the teacher isn't looking. You're the meanie who snatches a kid's lunch bag and tosses it around over his head and then slams it to the ground and stomps it. You're the smart ass who makes a cruel comment in class and gets everybody laughing at some poor kid, and you're the jock in the locker room, jerking the class nerd's underwear painfully into his butt crack. I'll bet you're really looking forward to giving me a big mental wedgie, aren't you?

I sat silent and blank, returning his stare. He continued, "When you do make it to class, you're ill prepared and unshaven. Shoddy is the word I'd use."

I grinned. "I've heard that word before."

He nodded. "No doubt."

I leaned back in the chair and crossed my leg. "What about crappy? Think that one applies, too?"

Smiley gave me a puzzled look. The reprimand wasn't going as he'd planned, and he began to sense that I was one nerd who wasn't going to timidly pick Fruit of the Looms out of my ass crack. He stepped his attitude up a notch.

"I refuse to bandy words with you, mister. We made a mistake in adding you to our faculty." He was tossing my job in the air, a symbolic bag lunch. I tightened my fingers on the chair arms and said nothing.

Then, he dropped my job and stomped it. "I won't drag this out any longer. You're fired. Find another position for which you're better suited, perhaps as a photographer for a newspaper, where a scruffy appearance would be an asset."

"Scruffy? That's a new one."

He got up from behind his desk and held his office door open for me. He said, "Fortunately, the school year's almost over. I'll let you finish out the week while we arrange for a substitute, but after that, we don't need your kind around here."

Apparently, Smiley was suddenly very afraid of me. He gripped the doorknob and made sweeping gestures toward the hall outside.

"Good luck somewhere else. That will be all. Get out. Now."

For the first time, a bully was afraid of me. Amazing! I walked out grinning.

It wasn't until I was in the parking lot that the implication of what had happened hit me. I'd been viciously fired. I didn't know what to do because I'd never been kicked off a job before. My legs were weak and I was a bit nauseated. I sat behind the wheel and tried to think it through, but I couldn't get my mind around it. I went home and told Marilyn that my teaching position was gone. She said she wondered what had taken the principal so long. I hadn't expected her to take it well, but I didn't think she'd actually side with the enemy. I went into the bathroom and threw up.

I was uncommonly exhausted by the shock of being fired, so I didn't go back to finish out the week. My assistant Elmer covered for me in the photo lab while I spent my days in bed, whiskered and greasy, listening to the planes overhead and waiting in vain for Trixie to return. A fine powder of plaster sifted from the ceiling onto the bedspread.

Marilyn soon began disappearing for hours at a time. She said she was looking for Trixie, but I think she was simply unable to watch her house and her husband fall apart. I sent my mind out, trying to find the mystical accord that Marilyn and I had known since childhood, but I registered only the dismal vacancy of her discontent.

It turned out that her disappearances had a purpose completely unrelated to Trixie. She'd been making secret arrangements with an attorney, and she suddenly presented me with divorce papers. Before I even knew what was happening, Marilyn had the decree drawn up and handed it to me over breakfast. For the second time, I was being viciously dismissed. Under "Grounds for Divorce" was typed *Irreconcilable Differences*, as though our marriage consisted of mismatched electrical circuitry and faulty plumbing.

Compared to this, losing my job was a minor setback. I've heard people say that they never knew what hit them, but I'd never fully appreciated those sentiments. I begged. I pleaded. When nothing worked, I yelled, "The collapsing house, the planes, the noise, they're all excuses! You simply want to leave me, not the house—me! Because I'm a fat nerd, a slob, a hopeless geek, right? Just admit it. What does this mean, *Irreconcilable Differences?*"

"It means you're crazy and I'm not. I want to sell this dump and you won't. Your appearance has nothing to do with it, Bill. Give me some credit. You've always looked like this and I've always loved you in spite of it, but now you're acting like a child. I'm an adult married to a childish, stubborn man, so I'm going to follow Trixie's example and leave this sinking ship."

"Oh, you're the adult here and I'm just your dumpy childhood sweetheart, so you can throw me out with the headless Barbie dolls and the rusty trikes and the puzzles with missing pieces, just an ugly broken toy that you've outgrown."

I snatched the papers and, without even looking, scrawled my signature across the bottom, glaring at Marilyn the whole time. I tossed them back to her. She tucked the papers into her handbag and headed for the door, crunching over chunks of fallen plaster. "When you decide to sell, call me at my mother's."

She took the old blue Datsun and left me the SUV that had three years of payments still owing. She drove straight to the courthouse where a judge inscribed the divorce documents that very afternoon, making it official. A grim process server knocked on the door, delivering my copy. Marilyn had given the creepy fellow fifty bucks so she wouldn't have to face me again.

I SPENT THE next few days in a darkroom I'd set up in the guest bath, printing countless pictures of Marilyn's smiling face. My assistant Elmer came to check on me.

"Man, you look terrible! Old lady bailed on you, huh?"

Elmer picked up a photograph. "Is this her? Wow, she's pretty. Well, I admire you for standing up for your convictions. Wanna go out for some pizza?"

He ducked his head when Mad Dog engines suddenly roared overhead, shaking the house and filling the air with plaster dust.

"JEEZ! DUDE! What's that horrible noise? Is that one of those planes?"

"Go home, Elmer. I need to make a phone call."

"Sure thing."

I'd developed a habit of calling Marilyn at her mother's every day, just to check in. For some reason I couldn't eat or sleep until I'd heard her voice. "Are you going to sell?" she asked each time I called. "No," I said, five days in a row.

When Elmer left I dialed the number, but she slammed down the phone as soon as she heard my voice. Later in the day, I tried again. A recording said that the number was changed and unlisted. The cold, impartial communication reminded me of Marilyn's voice saying *I'm not happy*, a terminal message against which there was no argument. I looked around at the pictures of Marilyn staring at me from every surface and I began to cry without making a sound.

Later, I was standing at the kitchen counter reading the instructions on a microwave dinner when the evening plane to Atlanta roared overhead. The house shook and the lights blinked out, never to return. I was in darkness, the only living being on a street of eerie abandoned houses, as I stood in my wrecked kitchen with the cold food carton in my hand.

The next morning there was banging on the front door because the doorbell didn't work. Blinking and grizzled, I opened the door and saw Mr. Box standing on a week's worth of newspapers on the front step. A hot summer wind lifted Box's thin patch of hair.

"Whatcher want?" I growled, blocking the doorway.

"May I come in?" Box pushed past me into the hot living room. "Air conditioning quit working, Bill? Oh . . . I see . . . no electricity. A pity, but predictable."

I gave him a bloodshot look as I dabbed at my forehead with a bathrobe sleeve. Box shoved plaster dust, dirty socks, and photographs of Marilyn off a chair, plopped down, and popped the locks of the briefcase on his lap.

"Look, Bill, we've been watching. We know your wife left. That's a lot of pain and suffering on your part and hers, too. The government wants this problem resolved and they're willing to be incredibly generous. The highest offer in this neighborhood was three times market value to Mrs. Finch. You're the last holdout, so you win. We're prepared to offer you four times market. It's a record offer, by the way. You're going to get over eight hundred thousand for this wreck of a house. On top of the eight hundred thousand, we're paying off your mortgage, so it's all pure profit. Congratulations, you're a rich man! Eight hundred thousand, Bill. That's a lot of smackers."

Just like that, my legs were noodles. "Eight hundred thousand?"

"Yep, plus the balance of the mortgage, so you're approaching a million dollar payoff, all clear profit. Tax free, I might add, because we've made arrangements with the IRS. You don't have to claim capital gains. Big, big bucks, you lucky dog. Just sign here and here."

What did it matter if I owned a home if Marilyn wasn't there to share it? A wise man knows when to throw in the towel, and here were almost a million reasons to do precisely that. I took Box's pen and scribbled my name across the lines.

"You know, I loved this house," I said as I returned the pen.

"I know, Bill," Box said kindly, and handed me the check. "You'll notice the check's in your name alone because you got the house in the divorce settlement. Don't worry about paperwork, the deed and such. We'll handle that part. By this time tomorrow, this house will be leveled along with all the others, and it'll be as though they never existed."

"As though they never existed," I echoed, and shook my head.

My wife was gone, my home, my job, my neighbors, my pride, my self-control, even my dog. It was as though I was the one who'd never existed.

I stared at the check, all those zeros, as Box rattled on. "I've taken the liberty of securing some movers for you. They'll be here this afternoon, so I suggest you spend the morning finding a place to go. Here's a list of nice rentals on the market, I'm sure you'll find a suitable place close to the high school. Oops, I forgot. You lost that job, didn't you?"

Box laid a consoling hand on my shoulder. "Why don't you call Marilyn at her mother's and tell her it's settled."

My head jerked up. "How'd you know she's with her mother?"

Box smiled inscrutably.

I gave him a pained look. "I can't call. I don't have her new number."

Box dug in his pocket and handed me a slip of paper. "Here. It's unlisted, but she gave it to us. I told her I was on my way to see you and she's waiting for your call. I'm sure she'll take you back because she never really wanted the divorce in the first place. She only did it as an incentive to force you to sell. She came to us with the idea of divorcing you and asked us to expedite the divorce through the courts. It was for everybody's good. It's all Marilyn's plan, and it worked quite well, I thought."

I stared at him, slack-faced. It was as though a cold wind had blown through my hot living room. I swayed and felt slightly faint. I whispered, "All of you were in on this? Even Marilyn?"

Box waved his hand. "Oh, we've been working with her behind the scenes. We sped up the divorce and Marilyn herself negotiated the high price for the house. Don't look so glum Bill, she always planned to come back once we'd forced some sense into you."

I flopped on the sofa and looked up at Box. "This was her manipulation? I never picked up on it. All my life I've believed I could read her mind."

"Clever girl, isn't she?" Box grinned.

"She was always smarter than me, even when we were kids." I looked again at the check in my hand. All those zeros started to blur. I never noticed when Box let himself out.

I took out my cell phone and dialed the number Box had given me. Marilyn answered on the first ring. "Hello? Bill?"

I sat speechless, breathing into the receiver.

"I know it's you, Bill. I can hear your adenoids."

I whispered, "Is it true? It was all a trick? The divorce?"

"Oh, don't be that way," she said. "It's like that game we played when we were kids, the one where we stared at each other. I could always make you blink first. You just blinked first again, that's all."

I blinked involuntarily as I held the receiver to my ear. "I can't talk any more," I mumbled, "I've got so much to do." I pressed the button to disconnect, and then I dialed my assistant, Elmer. "Can you help me pack? No, I didn't give up, exactly, I guess you could say I blinked."

Over the next hour, Elmer and I made quick work of packing some clothes, my laptop, and my camera bag (I left everything else for the wrecking ball). The phone rang repeatedly, but I ignored it. I slid the check into my pocket. All those zeros wouldn't support me forever in the Alps, but they'd last long enough for me to take some pictures of a place where flatness and sameness were novelties. I planned to set my feet on an imposing mountaintop that wouldn't shrug me off without a thought. Or a blink.

Suddenly, I was really hungry. Ravenous. I pictured a big

cheeseburger. I thought about apple pie. "Let's get something to eat, my treat." I said to Elmer.

I stood in the middle of the room and looked about. Elmer asked, "Something still bugging you?"

"Yeah. It just occurred to me. If she comes back, I'll be gone. She won't know where to find me."

"Who? Your wife?"

"No, Trixie, my dog. My wife can burn in hell."

THE MARKET PRICE

"Dogs are better than human beings
because they know but do not tell."
~Emily Dickinson

As JACK SMILEY, principal of St. Bernard High and productive member of the community, I stay on top of events that could affect my life and career. Just this evening I sat in front of my TV and watched the uproar about same-sex marriage. You may wonder how this distressing issue could impact the work of a normal, happily married educator and citizen such as myself.

Well, I'll tell you, and you'll be wise to pay attention to me.

This constant, relentless homosexual hue and cry, their unreasonable demands, the pretense of normalcy; all of these issues crept into my very office and landed squarely in my lap, ushered in by a certain Miss Lillian Fowler who, for many years, was an English teacher on my faculty. She turned out to be, as the common folk say, "a gator in the logs," namely a dangerous aberration, hidden in plain sight.

She was an ugly woman, but her homeliness served her well, helping her to float below the radar. She appeared to be a simple middle-aged spinster, physically unremarkable except for being quite tall for a woman. The students liked her well enough because she was fair in testing and lenient in grading. She was also something of a crusader and given to soap box rants. Perhaps her zeal was hormonal because she had, it was said, an over-dearth of inappropriate hormones and a dislike for appendages, particularly those that were intrusive, but it didn't stop her from sticking her nose into everybody's business. She was opinionated and tiresome in the forum of the faculty lounge. I found every excuse to avoid her.

Away from school, she was a member of a religious sect that went into the bayou every August to Christianize indigenous little heathens by use of a bible bus. I say good luck on those conversions. I'm as devout as the next fellow, hardly ever miss a Sunday, but I've always called exception to her righteous mania. Lillian Fowler twisted her sticky sweet beliefs like taffy around little rednecks who were, God knows, nothing but low class trash with none of the refinement of the educated and sophisticated working class. Her candy coating did the little hicks a disservice, but then Miss Fowler's whole life was simply a sugary glaze over a rotten, secret core.

As you've probably guessed, for the first four decades of her life, Miss Fowler operated in and out of a closet lined with Fowler money. She was insulated by her family's fortune. We called Miss Fowler an old maid because most of us weren't comfortable with the term "lesbian," a label with militant undertones. People didn't dwell on Miss Fowler (don't ask, don't tell) and saw past her variations because she rested in the cockles of family wealth. In my experience, the American elite are never held as accountable as the unbestowed. The lax temperament and sloth of the rich can be marked off to the taint of too much free time unencumbered by the demands of earning a living wage.

You and I know that the middle class isn't held in moral check by laws, discretion, personal creed, timidity or even religion. Your average man would be more assertive about his personal quirks and deviances if it weren't for one restraining factor, namely money. People suppress abnormal tendencies because they literally can't afford to do otherwise. They need their jobs. That's just my opinion, but I'm sure I'm right.

I'm in my second marriage. My first wife was schizophrenic, so I'm no stranger to unmanageable women. Mental illness aside, I find pushy women repulsive, and I must say Miss Fowler had a way of asserting her iron will like a Sumo wrestler. Over time, even her sexual perversion became uninteresting because it was too domesticated and lacked flair and spontaneity. Miss Fowler set up housekeeping with dull little Ophelia Rogers, our school librarian, in the mansion Miss

Fowler inherited as part of her cushy endowment. I always called Ophelia Rogers "Timid Ophelia," not to her face, of course. It's said that even Timid Ophelia found Miss Fowler tiresome and grew weary of Miss Fowler's multitude of standpoints and resented taking a knee to opinionated dictatorship. I'd imagine that Ophelia bit her lip and crept into the kitchen to feed that obese little dog of hers every time Miss Fowler got resolute.

In the end, Miss Fowler's opinions and money couldn't save her from the whim of fate. She developed terminal cancer and resigned from the classroom and began a downward spiral of hospitalizations. Ophelia, the faithful little thing, found strength to stand by her, to keep their lives in order, and never missed a day's work at the school. There are some people you must admire, even though you look for a reason not to do it, and I'll admit Ophelia won my admiration for her unswerving loyalty. But I withdrew my approval of her when the community came crashing down around her head because of the type of insidious propaganda she'd infiltrated onto the shelves of our school library.

The scandal broke after the advent of Miss Fowler's cancer, when Ophelia was struggling to hold it together, working days and caring for the dying Miss Fowler in the evenings. We enrolled a new freshman student, a congressman's daughter. This child was one of those demure types who favored corduroy jumpers and lacy collars and had her mother buy her feminine hygiene products because she was too shy to do it. The young lady was so lonely that she fell in with the outcast teenagers from the bayou, very bad company, indeed. They were the children of drug dealers and poachers and gun runners. I venture to guess that she found appeal in the pull of a fringe social class with secrets to keep. Those hellions opened her eyes to the narrowness of her world and introduced her to variations of individuality that she carried to extremes, even by swamp standards.

Two months after school started, she buzz cut her hair over her ears and bleached the remaining strands white and raccooned her eyes with black makeup. She donned platform shoes, revealing leather outfits, and what appeared to be a dog collar with studs. The shy wallflower stepped into the world reinvented as a rebel slut. Her parents could hardly recognize her. That neo-butch daughter sat at her parent's dinner table and opened a mouth that was slathered in purple lipstick and quoted the reclusive poet Emily Dickinson, who had been, in the congressman's opinion, possibly a closet lesbian. His daughter, whose name had gone from Samantha to Sam, had gained a stud-pierced tongue, but lost defining syllables and she lisped that she'd been turned on to Emily Dickinson by that crusading school librarian, Ophelia Rogers. Ophelia had recognized the same introverted tendencies in Samantha that were said to be in the withdrawn Emily Dickinson, and Ophelia pointed out the nature of their kindred spirits.

The parents quickly grasped the reference and the possibility that their daughter could be innocently drawn into those same sexually deviant pathways that (rumor has it) were walked by Emily Dickinson, and certainly trod by Ophelia Rogers. In retaliation, the congressman and his wife turned their gun sights on the librarian. They appeared to be enormously relieved to be presented with a hook on which to hang their parental frustrations.

Faster than the congressman could say *perversion,* he showed up at a school board meeting and informed the board members that they had a snake in their little garden of knowledge and the reptile was offering the kind of information that God-fearing young women had no business knowing. He presented evidence obtained through a private detective. He laid bare for the school board the particulars of the intimate life of Ophelia Rogers, such as it was, although it certainly wasn't a community secret. Any member of the board could have told him quite outright how Ophelia got her ashes hauled. The board told him that they would take his disclosures under advisement and he reminded them, on his way out, that they were all government employees and servants of the people and there wasn't one among them above a full and through investigation, including a scathing tax audit.

He then sent for his posse of congressional aides and they took up a room in the courthouse and organized a committee of local puckered conservatives to review our school's library books. Soon all sorts of accusations were flying and whole sections of shelves were denuded. Those offending books were boxed and taped securely and initialed by the councilman himself, which was tantamount to pitching them into a bonfire.

I'm an educator, after all, and I thought that the banning of certain established classics on their long list was rather excessive, but I was only recently tenured and no fan of IRS audits, so I shut my door and divorced myself from the banning process. I was given the choice of protesting the symbolic book burning or throwing Ophelia on the fire along with the books, so I'd opted for roasting Ophelia because she did, in a fashion, ask for it, don't you think?

Having dealt with the lesbian-leaning books, the congressman then turned his sights on the lesbian librarian herself. He took his daughter to a therapist who told him that children who have been sexually traumatized often exhibit irrational, outlandish, attention-seeking behavior, and the tongue stud certainly qualified as irrational. Upon hearing this, the congressman became convinced that Ophelia had probably behaved inappropriately with his daughter and he pressured, bullied, and harassed the child into a confession. The more she denied it, the more he became convinced he was right, because denial, according to the therapist, would be her initial reaction. Finally, lacking the evidence to take legal steps, he went instead to the school board where he spread out his distressing resolution in full, and demanded knee-jerk justice.

It wasn't long before the ruination of Ophelia Rogers was fully realized. The gentle lady was called, trembling, before the puppet school board. They informed her that the school no longer required her services. Moreover, her influence was not to be tolerated. Even her transitory presence would not be welcome at any school in the district, nor near any playground, center, or recreation building where children gathered.

At the congressman's urging, the religious community got involved in branding Ophelia. A local preacher stood on the steps of the school board building and held a candlelight vigil that escalated into a literary exorcism. The newspaper covered it and anyone who hadn't already heard about Ophelia and Miss Fowler were made fully aware of the fact that God hates queers.

The deacons at Miss Fowler's church subsequently suggested that

Miss Fowler should boot Ophelia out of her house. If she didn't, Miss Fowler would be required to stop conducting her missionary work with the swamp heathens. Miss Fowler, chemo-bald and too sick to be a missionary to anybody, held her beloved Bible to her bosom as Ophelia pushed her wheelchair out of the church that Miss Fowler's money had helped to build. The two of them went into seclusion in the mansion, and even their fat little dog was no longer seen in the garden.

At the end of the school year, the congressman took his daughter out of our school and sent her to an exclusive boarding school up north where there was a vigilant staff and a strict dress code. Then he and his wife bought a house at the beach and they moved out of town and haven't been seen around these parts, except during the last election, at which time he came to town to campaign as a crusader for the underdog.

Things eventually quieted down, and then one day a limousine pulled up to the Fowler mansion and Miss Fowler was driven to a hospice facility to die in style with Ophelia and the fat dog by her side. They established residence in a lovely, posh hospital upstate for a few weeks until Miss Fowler finally expired. Her body was returned to St. Bernard for burial in the ancestral tomb, and I attended the quiet funeral out of common decency. Ophelia delivered a eulogy to those few who showed up. She extolled Miss Fowler's endless virtues and I wasn't a bit surprised when she looked out over those in attendance and concluded her little speech with these lines from Miss Fowler's favorite Emily Dickinson poem:

I took one draught of life, I'll tell you what I paid,
Precisely an existence, the market price, they said.

IN TIME, THE last will and testament of Miss Fowler was carried out and Ophelia Rogers became a rich woman, even by the congressman's standards. Miss Fowler had willed a stretch of property by the interstate to Ophelia and she promptly leased it as a site for a new super discount store. As so often happens, the discount store put several local mom-and-pop shops out of business, just as Ophelia planned. She set up a tax shelter and became even richer.

And then, suddenly, the Fowler mansion burned down. The source of the fire remains a mystery to this day, but arson isn't out of the question. A lot of people were in strained circumstances because of the superstore strangulation of local businesses, so it's not out of the question that they took a little Molotov justice. Their attempt at revenge only served to make Ophelia even richer because the mansion was fully insured, building and contents. Considering all the memories that the mansion held, I'm sure Ophelia wasn't overly bothered by the fact that she no longer had to live there alone. After the mansion burned, Ophelia closed her accounts and moved out of state with her dog. She saw to it that none of her money stayed locally to benefit the town in any way except for an endowment to the local animal shelter.

AT THE BEGINNING of the next academic year, the school board engaged a new librarian, Mrs. Comstock, a chubby, smiling, non-controversial married lady with a house full of children. One of her first acts was to quietly bring the boxes of books out of storage and put them back on the shelves, where those banned books had a new surge of popularity. This renewed interest in the controversial writings ultimately proved the congressman's daughter had been correct when she went off the decorous deep end and showed us that there's nothing like a touch of infamy for getting noticed. All the books are back in circulation now, including the poetic works of the morose Miss Dickinson.

Behind the shield of my office, I observed the actions of the new librarian. I expected some mild objection to her restocking the shelves with the formerly forbidden books, but it seemed that nobody in town was going to object in any way. When I was sure of the public's acceptance of her actions, I stuck my neck out and gave the new librarian my full support. It was the least I could do.

AN INCIDENT OF GRAVITY

"Happens to everybody.
Horses, dogs, men.
Nobody gets out of life alive."
~Irving Ravetch

THE DEATH OF Agnes Watts was in the cards. You didn't need a crystal ball to know that she'd been digging her grave with a knife and fork for years. Well, today the symbolic axe fell and Agnes dropped like a ton of bricks in the middle of the Holy Messenger Methodist pot-luck picnic in the church recreation hall. My sister Glenda and I saw it happen, so later that afternoon Glenda showed up at my house to hash it over, like a football coach grilling the team after a losing game.

I poured two cups of coffee and said, "I'm glad Agnes never knew what hit her. Dropped like a rock, a really big rock. Or a boulder, one of those giant boulders that rolls down a cliff and blocks both lanes of a highway."

Glenda was pacing with her hands behind her back. "Tina, her vacancy's going to be hard to fill," she speculated. "Who'd ever think we'd be a congregation with a theatrical problem?"

Every Christmas for many years, our congregation had assembled a live Nativity scene on the front lawn of the church. It was always a customary display of Mary, Baby Jesus, Joseph, shepherds, Wise Men, and an angelic third grader in a white sheet and coat hanger halo suspended by ropes over the scene, anchored to a deer hunter's tree stand decorated with palm fronds.

Agnes had played the part of the Virgin Mary for fourteen years, but as she got fatter and swelled progressively, she literally presented an overwhelming problem. Each Christmas, she took up more and more of the small stable, eventually crowding out the cotton batting sheep and the human shepherds, who were required to take their sheep and participate from the far side of a hedge as though they'd lost their way.

The deacons discussed enlarging the stable, but decided against it for the sake of authenticity, as if anybody really knew the size of the original stable. They said it should remain a stable, not a barn, which would be larger, but being born in a barn is not a desirable beginning, even in a seasonal reenactment. Moreover, there was concern about a subliminal message. The deacons feared that the community might conclude that Methodists thought of Mary as a mountain of flesh or a cartoonish slob or even a monstrous glutton. The dilemma literally loomed larger every Christmas.

"Food made her fat and happy and killed her at the same time, just like those people who climb mountains and freeze to death," Glenda said, waxing philosophical.

I said, "I'd hate to tell St. Peter that I choked on a mouthful of fried chicken, but heaven knows, it's a miracle nobody at the church has done it before, considering how they swarm the food table like mosquitoes at a love-in."

Glenda agreed with me about the overzealous eaters. On the day Agnes died, the crowd had been crouched like track runners waiting for the gun while they endured an extremely inclusive grace by the Reverend Jerome Smalls, a colorless little vicar able to throw a wet blanket the entire length of a room. When Jerome finished his blessings, forgivenesses, illnesses, bereavements, adversities, surgeries, shut-ins, and advertisers in the church bulletin, he said "A" and before he could add "men" the holy tsunami of parishioners surged the buffet table.

There was elbow jostling and spoon rattling as the congregation loaded their plates with green bean casserole and pasta salad and quivering Jell-O suspending grated carrots and cloudy fruit cocktail. Mostly they were going for the fried chicken that Kitty had brought on her best gold-rimmed china platter. The folks down the line prayed, not against adversities, but in the hope the chicken wouldn't run out.

If Agnes had known she was minutes from death, she probably would've displayed better manners, but she was mercifully oblivious to her impending doom as she focused on filling her plate with her last meal, as fate would have it. She elbowed through the line and stuck her pudgy hand between the belly of one parishioner and the backside of another and blindly scored a wishbone so succulent it could've been a gift of the Magi. She huffed and waddled to a table, plopped down her brimming plate, and lowered her wide load onto a creaking chair that was only a pound or two from buckling. Pinkies extended, she daintily lifted the wishbone and crunched into the moist flesh and crisp skin.

Helen Smalls, the insufferable wife of the Reverend, was sitting at the other end of the table. Helen is one of those snobby dames born with her face lifted, and entitled to more air and sunlight than the rest of us. Everybody has a good word for Helen, and they all whisper it. Helen chose that moment to make a snide and very loud remark about the size and shape of Agnes.

I now said to Glenda, "I still can't believe Helen said that. What a witch. She's gotten even worse since she became a blond."

"A blond? She wishes," Glenda said with a curl in her upper lip that she uses to great effect when her bridgework is in. "She's no blond. She's a cross between a brunette and a drug store."

I dipped a macaroon into my coffee. "Doesn't help. Her face still looks like it wore out five bodies."

Glenda said, "Yeah, and she uses her mouth like a murder weapon."

"Exactly what did she say about Agnes?" I prompted.

"She said Agnes should shop for new Virgin Mary robes at Brent's Sporting Goods because they were having a sale on tents."

When Helen had made this remark, everybody at the picnic table stopped eating and looked down the table at Agnes in the hope that her vigorous chewing had dulled her hearing. Alas, Agnes heard the fateful remark and her eyes focused on Helen through puffy lids and flaps and folds of facial fat. Her cheeks twitched, quivered, and flushed bright red from the first double chin on up. She opened her fingers and the gnawed wishbone bounced on her plate and came to rest in coleslaw. Alice drew a breath to defend herself and as it turned out, it was her last. Her eyes widened even more as the half-chewed bite of chicken, soft and slick with spit, slid down her throat and wedged in her windpipe. She grabbed the edge of the table and pulled herself to her feet and the flesh of her feet bubbled over the tops of her shoes. The chair, freed of its ponderous burden, crashed to the floor in relief. Agnes clutched her throat. "Gakk-k-k!"

"She's choking!" screamed Reverend Smalls.

He ran behind Agnes and threw his arms around her middle but his hands were about a foot and a half short of meeting in front.

"Oh dear," he mumbled.

Agnes wobbled and toppled backward, taking the Reverend with her like a squirrel in a falling tree. He rolled clear just before impact. Agnes hit the floor with a thud that reverberated through Holy Messenger backsides on benches for three tables around.

At first, screams and gasps of the crowd filled the air, but then they grew quiet and a tomb-like hush fell over the scene. Mrs. Snell, who worked as a dog groomer in a veterinarian office, came cautiously forward and took Agnes's pulse and pronounced Agnes to be dead, to the best of her knowledge of Airedales.

An ambulance was summoned, and as they waited, eyewitnesses discussed the cause of death, namely Kitty's chicken. Since her covered dish dealt the death blow, Kitty took the situation to heart and went into an alert faint. She sprawled on a picnic table and placed a wet paper towel across her own eyes.

Soon, the ambulance whined up and two attendants, Jake and Arliss, jumped out. Arliss was a local boy, but Jake's family moved here when he was two years old, so he was only a "resident" and could never be a "native." After thirty years of residency, Jake had only recently gotten beyond "inhabitant."

The third attendant, a new trainee, threw open the rear doors of the ambulance and bounded out like the vehicle was filled with vipers. His name was Petey and he had a head of hair so thick, red and crimped, it was as though somebody had unraveled a wool sweater on his head. His face was an acne war zone. It was his first day on the job, and Jake asked him why he hadn't brought the gurney.

Petey asked, "The whut?"

Jake filled his cheeks with air and blew and said it was the table bodies lie on.

"That thing like an ironing board on wheels?" Petey asked.

Jake sighed, "Boy, if they ever put a price on your head, take it. Go figure it out."

Petey scurried to the ambulance. Willett Orso, who's so ancient his ears are the size of palmetto leaves, said with the soft, round vowels of a southern gentleman, "Looka that boyee run."

They all turned to look, including Kitty, because curiosity overrode apoplexy, so she propped on one elbow and lifted a corner of the paper towel to watch the boyee until Petey disappeared behind the church, at which time Kitty flopped down and resumed fainting where she'd left off.

"Where's the patient?" Jake asked Reverend Smalls. The Reverend pointed and said, "Gentlemen, she's beyond being a patient. Maybe a client or patron, even a customer. I don't know exactly what to call her."

After a brief examination, Jake stood and flexed his back. "Call her an incident." In Jake's world, all dead bodies were incidents.

Banging and swearing came from the ambulance, and then Petey hurried up with the gurney. Jake said, "Petey, slow down. Can't you see you're rolling over toes? Boy, if you said what you thought, you'd be speechless."

Petey, Jake, and Arliss stood motionless, studying the body of Agnes. Arliss asked, "You want me to fetch it?"

Petey asked, "Fetch whut?"

Jake circled Agnes, heel-toe, heel-toe, arms out for balance, carefully measuring the dimensions of the incident. Arliss watched him and asked again, "Jake? You want me to fetch it?"

Jake dipped his head in a tight nod and said, "Yeah, you better fetch it."

Arliss ran toward the ambulance.

Once again, Petey asked, "Fetch whut?"

Jake's time-consuming assessment had given everybody the opportunity to pull up chairs. They passed chips and balanced cartons of dip on their knees. Iced tea and soft drinks were handed out. When everybody had their refreshments, Arliss solved the mystery of what he was fetching. He ran up with a Polaroid camera. Jake took it in hand and snapped a photograph of Agnes and the camera spit the picture out with a competent whir. Jake laid the snapshot on a table and the congregation crowded around to look at it. The Polaroid was as milky as a blind man's eyes, but soon an image of Agnes surfaced. Reverend Smalls squinted and said, "My, doesn't she look life-like?"

Willett Orso said, "Jerome, she looks like a dead whale on a beach."

Jerome asked, "Why are you taking pictures? Agnes wouldn't like that."

Jake said, "These pictures are for legal stuff and such, to prove what we were up against, if any damage occurs, I mean."

"I don't know how she could get more damaged than this," the Reverend said.

Jake replied, "Damage to us. In case we hurt our backs or need disability leave for something that got sprained or sprung. We take pictures of all, uh, large incidents."

Before he took the second Polaroid, Jake told Petey, "Get in the picture."

Petey raked his fingernails down his acne and asked, "How come?"

Jake said, "For perspective."

Petey squatted next to Agnes with his arms resting on his knees. As an afterthought, he reached up and smoothed his hair that was standing out like a red dandelion. Jake snapped the second picture and pocketed them both and the boys got down to the ponderous business of transporting the incident that was Agnes.

Following a hasty tactical discussion, Jake stood at Agnes's head while Arliss and Petey positioned themselves at her feet. They made a vein-popping attempt to lift Agnes onto the collapsed gurney, but her limber condition combined with her weight led to the elevation of her extremities but not her middle, which never broke contact with the floor, but only jiggled. The three of them bent with their palms on their knees and panted.

"I've never been so acutely aware of gravity in my life," said Jake.

"How about we roller?" asked Arliss.

"We can't roll her all the way to the ambulance," said Jake.

"She'll get all dirty and scratched up."

Arliss said, "No, I mean we jam the gurney up against the side of her so we can roller onto it stead of lifting her. Petey can brace it from sliding, and you and me'll push like holy hell till she flops over onto it."

Jake said, "Won't work. If we flip her, she'll be face down on the gurney. That embalmer at the funeral parlor's gonna laugh if we bring him an incident face down. I'm sick of him making jokes about us."

Arliss said, "Ah, he laughs at everything. Helluva sense of humor."

Petey had been quiet, but suddenly spoke up. "Do a two-stepper. Flopper over on the floor first, so as she's face down, then flopper onto the mashed-down gurney so as she's face up."

Jake and Arliss stared at Petey. "Well, outta the mouths of babes," said Jake.

Jake and Arliss knelt along the side of Agnes. They worked their hands under her as far as they could decently reach, and Jake called, "One-two-three-FLIP!" The guys grunted and Agnes flopped over onto her stomach. The impressed congregation breathed, "Owww."

Petey got beside the collapsed gurney on his knees and jammed it against the side of Agnes. He hunkered down and braced it while Jake and Arliss pushed and grunted again and flipped Agnes onto the gurney face up. Everybody sighed, "Ahhh." There was a smattering of applause. Some of the congregation shook hands or high-fived.

With grunting effort and the help of several parishioners, the boys extended the legs of the gurney and covered Agnes with two sheets because one didn't do it. Their next chore was the pronouncement of death that had yet to be performed by an authority with a license. The coroner didn't go out on Sunday, so the boys decided to stop at his house to ask him to sign off that Agnes had no further business with anybody on this earthly sphere except for the embalmer with the sense of humor.

Agnes was rolled out the door and onto the blacktop and around the corner of the church. The congregation rushed to the top of the driveway, which had quite a steep downward grade to the street. They arrived in time to see the boys and the gurney picking up speed down the incline, aided by gravity and rain-slicked blacktop. Halfway down, the boys broke into a run behind the gurney that had pulled ahead of them.

Jake shouted, "Petey, run ahead and open the back doors!"

Petey got to the ambulance barely in time to throw open the doors and jump clear as the gurney hit the ambulance with a thud that caused the siren to emit a short whine. If it had been anyone other than Agnes, the body would've slid off the gurney and into the ambulance unaided, but being Agnes, she stayed solidly put.

Jake and Arliss ran up and collapsed the legs of the gurney and pushed it, along with its burden, into the ambulance. Petey jumped in the back as nimble as a spider monkey with raindrops sparkling in his hair. Jake and Arliss slammed the back doors and hopped in the front, fired up the ambulance, waved out the windows, and headed off. They had the life-like Polaroids of Agnes stuffed in Jake's pocket and the great mound of Agnes herself in the back, insulted, strangled, flip-flopped, polarized, gurneyed, double-sheeted, sped-up, impeded, put into perspective, and finally stuffed in the vehicle with just enough room for a skinny red-haired trainee.

The crowd watched the ambulance and commented on the pretty red and white lights reflected in the puddles. After it turned the corner, there wasn't anything else to see, except rivulets of rain running into the gutters. A stifling cloud of melancholy settled over the picnic. The crowd was weary, heavy-limbed, bleary-eyed, glutted by too much stimulation. A few turned and shuffled away and soon others followed, listless and long-faced, monosyllabled, moving in a sluggish, bumping wave.

Reverend Smalls prompted the cleanup committee into action. Somebody tossed out Agnes's last meal, including Kitty's wishbone, the southern fried instrument of fate. A committee member picked up Agnes's big black purse and handed it to Reverend Smalls. He turned it over to his wife Helen for final disposition. The Reverend didn't think it was polite for a man to rifle through a lady's pocketbook, even if she was most recently, if not officially, an incident.

When everything was clean and in order, everybody left. Kitty completed her faint just in time for a volunteer take her home, but not before she had the presence of mind to grab her best gold rimmed china platter.

There are some things you just can't replace.

LITTLE PRECIOUS AND THE VIRGIN MARY PIE

"Flatterers look like friends, as wolves like dogs."
~George Chapman

REVEREND JEROME SMALLS of the Holy Messenger Methodist Church of St. Bernard Parrish was cringing in his office. Jerome was as immobilized as a turtle on its back, slow motion kicking. Sounds of singing drifted from the church next door. The choir was rehearsing their Christmas cantata, carols of inspiration and hope, but they did nothing to ease the Reverend's anxiety.

Jerome had always been an insightful theologian, but it didn't serve him very well in the practical world of everyday church life. The cocoon that was his musty office made such a comfortable hiding place that his ample backside had, over time, rubbed the plush off the seat cushion of his sagging chair. He doted on his familiar, moldy books and surrounded himself with water colors he'd painted, hanging on every available piece of wall, landscapes of faraway, exotic places he'll never visit. He'd copied them from photographs in the National Geographic magazine.

Jerome resented the pulpit because he thought it made him too conspicuous, and he avoided home because of his abrasive wife, Helen. She was a gossip without conscience. If half the town didn't know how the other half lived, it wasn't Helen's fault. Cars on the highway didn't run down as many people as Helen Smalls.

Jerome secretly likened himself to a butterfly, one of God's most delicate creatures, fluttering about aimlessly and easily crushed. He couldn't decide where courage came from, what organ or gland or bit of tissue. Not from the backbone, because crabs have no backbone, yet they're engineered for aggression with their claws and hard shells, rather like Helen. Courage couldn't come from the brain either, he reasoned, because he was a smart man, smarter than most, yet he couldn't think himself into acts of bravery. Lately, he didn't seem to be able to think correctly at all. He was, he realized, terrified of even the simplest things.

His current dilemma was Agnes, or rather the lack of her. She'd been the church tableau's official Virgin Mary for years, but Agnes had recently dropped dead at the church picnic and left a very large chair to fill. Helen had informed Jerome that she wanted to take over the role. What was he to do? He couldn't simply appoint his own wife. It wasn't proper. It wasn't democratic. It probably wasn't even Christian.

Helen's manipulation of the dilemma had been planned perfectly, to her way of thinking. By the time Agnes was finally in the ground, Christmas was only three weeks away, so there was a rush to fill the vacancy in time for rehearsals, such as they were. The players actually met so they could practice standing still, which was not as easy as it seemed in light of bugs, bodily functions, itches, coughs, and sneezes. Helen knew that Jerome would be forced to appoint an immediate replacement for Agnes. It was his duty, however distressful, and his duty alone. This was brought into sharp focus by Coach Bear Lonnier, who had always played the part of Joseph in the tableau. Bear was the local high school baseball coach, and he put the sentiments of the church deacons quite bluntly, in athletic terms. "For God's sake, man, get a life and join the team," he barked. "Inform Helen that she's not stepping into the part without giving others an equal chance at try-outs of some sort. She's not officially on the roster yet. There has to be a casting call and if she doesn't agree to compete for the part, she'll have to sit it out on the sidelines."

"I wouldn't even know how to begin to tell Helen something like that," Jerome whined.

"I'm sure you'll find the words, once the game's down to the wire," Bear said. "There's more than one way to skin a cat."

"Yes, but unfortunately some ways require more cooperation from the cat than would ordinarily be expected," Jerome said.

"See here, man, if you're not up to the challenge, the board will have to rethink your contract renewal."

Miracles happen everyday. Mothers lift wrecked cars off of trapped infants. People who can't swim somehow rescue the drowning. Beloved objects that were lost or stolen long ago suddenly turn up in unexpected places. Courage swells and spreads through the most timid of souls. And so it was with Jerome. He found a wellspring of inner fortitude. Perhaps the natural order of things strolled through the doorway of Jerome's theology and bolstered him up. He may have remembered Michelangelo, a painter like himself, under the thumb of a tyrannical Pope. Michelangelo blotted it all out with masterful swirls of color and found the fortitude to lie on his back on tall scaffolding, year after year, far removed from the Pope, shouting up from below.

Perhaps it was Christmas itself, a promise of joy and hope that gave Jerome courage. Most likely, it was the threat of unemployment. Whatever the source, Jerome recalled the location of his backbone. The very next Sunday, he stood in his pulpit, in full receivership of Helen's scalding glare from a pew below, and sent out an unexpected casting call to the congregation.

He said, "Agnes's untimely departure at the picnic, God rest her soul, has left a vacancy in our Nativity. We will miss her. Lord knows she was a predominant presence, but a new Virgin Mary must be chosen."

He added, "Interestedladiesseemeafterchurch." Then he quickly bowed his head, or in this case ducked it, and closed his eyes. "Let us pray."

He could still feel the radiation of Helen's wrath branded on his retinas.

A FEW DAYS passed, and aside from Helen, sedate little Marie Higgins was the only other candidate who came forward to apply for the role. Agnes had been Marie's best friend. Sweet, peace-loving Marie couldn't bear to see the part go to Helen, be she pastor's wife or not. Deep in her grave, Agnes would spin like a drill if that happened, so Marie gathered her nerve and threw her hat into the ring. This two-woman competition for the role dealt Reverend Smalls a sticky hand. Favoritism toward his unpopular wife would part the congregation like the Red Sea and displease the deacons, as well. On the other hand, he had to live with Helen, day after oppressive day.

When Helen learned that she had a rival for the role, she exploded, attacking Marie verbally from several angles, and even badmouthing Marie's small dog, Little Precious. "Nasty, yipping little monster," sneered Helen.

Jerome listened in persecuted silence and wondered how he would ever resolve the dilemma. Fortunately, Bear Lonnier stepped forward with an unorthodox suggestion. Being a baseball coach, Bear possessed keen insight into the manipulation of meager potential. He found the reverend slumped with a long face in his cluttered office.

"Look Jerome, all cards on the table." Bear was always laying all cards on the table for his baseball team. "You think you gotta give that role to Helen to keep peace at home, but there's folks in the church won't stand for it. We need a contest to take the selection out of your hands. But listen, it has to be an event Helen can't lose."

"You mean like some sort of sporting event?"

Bear was probably right. He was a coach and a sporting man after all, and he understood the intricacies of competition. Jerome pictured Helen running and sweating, straining and gasping, jumping over hurdles, pole vaulting, falling and staggering to her feet only to fall again, bloody and bruised. The image cheered him.

Bear said, "Nah, no sports. I'm talking about something Helen's good at."

"Something Helen's good at? Now let me see."

The reverend shifted in his chair. For years, he'd suffered from hemorrhoids aggravated by stress. That day, Jerome felt as though he were sitting on a hot grill. Humiliating, and unfair, he thought. He supposed there were Godless atheists walking around, sitting, driving, with perfectly comfortable backsides, while he, a devout Christian, had little demons going at his rear with hot pitchforks. But then, a man who'd lived with Helen Smalls for twelve years no longer questioned the fairness of life.

". . . good at?" Bear was asking a question.

"Huh?" Jerome was pulled from his reverie. He realized he'd been staring at a landscape on the wall, one of his own paintings, a tranquil tree-lined road that disappeared into the horizon.

"I said isn't there something Helen's good at?"

Jerome pondered. "She's a pretty fair cook."

"What's the best thing she makes?"

"Oh, well now, I'd have to say pecan pie. Best I ever ate."

"Well then, that's it. It's perfect. The Ladies' Christmas bake sale is next Sunday after church. Have a pecan pie competition between Helen and Marie as an accessory to the bake sale."

"You're not serious!"

"Why not? We'll get a couple of judges and clue them in ahead of time. Matter of fact, I'll volunteer to be one of the judges and I'll ask my friend Charlie LaForce to be the other judge, as an independent agent from outside the church, to cover all bases, so to speak. He's a Catholic, so they can't say he's biased, not about pie, anyway. We'll make sure Helen wins."

Jerome said, "Charlie LaForce? Isn't he that fellow with the talking dog?"

"You mean Lucky Jack? Yeah, he talks, so what?"

"I have to consider my reputation. A talking dog is a sticky wicket, theologically speaking. If a dog can talk, then a dog can think logically. If he can think logically, he can reason. If he can reason, he knows right from wrong and that means he has spiritual judgment. If he has spiritual judgment, he might have a soul. Animals with souls? This gets into the whole vegetarian, animal right-to-life thing. Like I say, it's a sticky wicket, theologically. Can't rile up the vegetarians. Those people are fond of holding protests and walking in picket lines."

Bear had been listening with his mouth hanging open. "What on God's green earth are you going on about? It's a crooked pie contest, Jerome. It ain't a vegetarian Armageddon. Get over it. Sometimes you're such a weenie, I swear."

"Talking dog aside, it's still unfair to poor Marie Higgins."

"You can't afford to be fair. You've got to throw the game or you'll never have another moment's peace at home. Helen's waited years to get her hooks in that role."

"I wish there was some other way."

"Jerome, would you rather have the ladies wrestle for it? I got the mats over at the high school. I could set it up."

Jerome hesitated.

"Reverend? Seriously? Holy Jesus, I was only joking."

"Sorry. You're right. I'll tell Helen . . . and I'll phone Marie, too."

The Reverend sighed and looked out the window through a curtain of rain. Cars swooshed past on the wet street. It had been steadily raining for a dreary winter week.

Within the walls of his home, Jerome called Helen "dearest" and "honey" and told her she was bound to win and nobody could say that she didn't get the part fairly. He didn't tell her the contest was fixed. That would imply doubt that she could win honestly. She raged that a competition was insulting. He winced and sighed. He told Helen she was going to win, no doubt at all, because she did everything so well. Helen said that Jerome was right, for once. Jerome said, "That's the spirit, sweetheart." Then he went to the phone to call Marie Higgins and tell her that she would have to compete in a bake-off.

"You want me to bake a pie?" Marie said into the receiver.

"Yes," said Smalls. "Pecan. A pecan pie."

"Is that even . . . proper?" Marie whispered into the phone.

"It's not sacrilege, Marie," Smalls explained. "It's pastry."

"Seems a bit . . . whimsical," said Marie, but she consented.

She hung up the phone and studied her Chihuahua, Little Precious, as the dog danced and jumped, a pup on springs and uppers. Marie detected the closing trap of a snow job settling softly and soundlessly around her.

"Something's going on, Precious—a plot. I can just feel it."

Precious tipped her head to one side, a cute manipulation of the smaller breeds. It melted Marie. She fetched the box of Doggie Doodles. The sight of the box sent Precious into a yipping frenzy. Marie sat on the floor and Precious self-catapulted into her lap. She hand-fed the dog, taking an occasional bite herself. "They're trying to shut me out," Marie told Precious, who only crunched and ignored her. "They're turning it into a contest. They think I'll back down, but I can't. I owe it to Agnes."

The following day, Helen held court at the checkout of Winn-Dixie, assaulting the ears of the church's choir director, who was behind her in line. "That Marie Higgins has no family, no depth, only that dreadful yippy dog she takes everywhere she goes."

Helen smoothed her hair. "I think I'll have my Virgin Mary costume made by a professional. After all, I'll be using it for years. Oh, wait! I have a coupon for that."

She fussed at the bag boy for crushing her buns and scolded the clerk about the prices, and even worked in her usual remark about the pitiful salary the church paid Jerome. After leaving the grocery, Helen parked down the block from a liquor store. Looking both ways, she slipped inside and bought a bottle of brandy. "For baking," she told the indifferent clerk. He shrugged as he punched the register keys. "Whatever."

Helen bug-eyed him. "You don't believe me?"

"Lady, I don't give a . . . darn." He dropped the bottle into a bag and held it out. Helen snatched it and scurried to her car, convinced that the clerk must be a heathen atheist.

Marie, meanwhile, haunted the baking aisle of the Walmart, bought ingredients, and made a pie, but it was runny and leathery. Precious refused to taste it. She made another pie that looked promising, but she dropped it. She sat at her kitchen table and cried bitter tears for herself and for her lost friend Agnes, and for the perfect pie that would never come out of her oven.

THE SUNDAY OF the contest sloughed in, dim and wet. Marie's final, contesting pie sat quivering, congealed and lumpy, a hostile pastry hunkering on the counter, sulking at its own existence. "You're an embarrassment to yourself," Marie said to the pie.

She called to Little Precious. The dog skittered up, in and out between Marie's feet. Partners in this familiar dance, they made their way to the car. Marie hid the surly pie in the trunk and put Precious in the front seat beside her. Blinking back tears, she turned the car in the direction of the church, thankful that Little Precious was going with her so she didn't have to make the trip alone.

In the Small's driveway, Helen yelled for the Reverend to hustle up. He shuffled out and dropped into the driver's seat with a wince, and they, too, made their way to the pastry showdown.

As other ladies of the church arrived, they carried their baked goods into the meeting hall. The dessert sale would be held after the service. Helen left her pie in the car because it deserved a grand entrance just before judging began. Helen's pie was magnificent, mounded, a golden creation sparkling with a thin crystalline coating of caramel over layers of brandied pecans.

Marie tried not to think about the miserable pie in her trunk. She petted Precious and left the dog in the car, then trudged into church and found a seat near the back. She spotted Helen in a front pew, wearing a lovely new hat. Jerome began his sermon entitled, "David versus Goliath in God's Arena of Faith."

The Reverend said, "David took a stone of Justice and flung it with a sling of Righteousness. With that act of faith, he defeated a giant. He *believed*, even though he was up against incredible odds. David believed in justice . . ."

Marie pictured the stone hitting Goliath squarely in the forehead. She saw the giant falling, falling, and imagined a shattering thud when he hit the ground, a cloud of dust rising around him. A possibility burst upon her consciousness, as though a stone had hit her in the head as well. She hardly noticed when the service was over.

She waited until the congregation shuffled out and the church was empty, then she stood up with her back straight and her chin up. She went to the parking lot. Helen was also in the parking lot, going to her own car to fetch her glorious pie. Helen was radiating confidence.

Standing at her car, Marie set in motion her own act of faith. Little Precious barked a greeting through the car window. Marie opened the door and let Precious out and the pup danced around Marie's feet. Marie stooped as David must have stooped when he picked up the stone. She steadied Precious, her hands cupping the dog's head, and whispered, "That lady has Doggie Doodles, Precious. Go get them. Go on, now."

Helen was walking from her car, skipping around rain puddles, her perfect pie balanced in her hands. Precious scampered over to Helen and began her usual dance, yipping and jumping, running between Helen's feet as Helen made a desperate effort to keep her balance.

Sometimes you know how a thing is going to play out, as David must've known when he felt the weight of the stone in his hand. In that brief suspension of probabilities, even as Goliath's shadow fell across him, David foresaw it all. Looking back, everyone agreed that it all seemed to happen in slow motion. First, Helen lost her footing on the wet asphalt. She pitched forward and her perfect pie flew out of her hands. A woman in the crowd outside the church screamed. A man darted out and made a valiant dive to catch the pie, but only tipped it with his fingers, causing it to spin upward as Helen slid down and landed on her stomach with a whoosh of expelled breath. The pie spun up and up until it reached its apex, hung in the air, and then descended fast, splatting on the ground several feet from Helen. She lifted her head from the pavement just in time for flying gobs of caramel filling and several airborne pecans to splatter her face and hair and lodge in the netting of her new hat.

"OOOOH SHIT! MY PIE!" Helen shrieked.

Observers gasped at her profanity, then fell silent and gaped at the pastor's wife on the pavement. The only sounds were her sobs and the slurps of Little Precious lapping caramel filling off the wet asphalt. Reverend Smalls appeared beside his wife. With gentle hands, he helped her to her feet and steered her toward his office.

"Come here, Little Precious!" Marie called across the parking lot. Precious wobbled up, already feeling woozy from the brandy in Helen's pie. Marie hustled the dog into the car.

Helen, uncharacteristically humbled by her profane outburst and her undignified sprawl in the parking lot, hid in Jerome's office until most of the congregation had gone, then she sulked home to bandage her skinned knees and wash pie out of her hair.

Marie's pie was the only entry in the contest, so the judges, Bear Lonnier and his friend Charlie LaForce, declared Marie to be the winner by forfeit. After a cursory look at the malignant pastry, they didn't bother tasting it. The church had its new Virgin Mary. Marie was smiling and gracious, and wasn't it too bad that Helen had taken that dreadful spill? The judges had no idea they were in the presence of a giant killer.

Marie took her four-legged conspirator home and treated her to all the Doggie Doodles she wanted. It seemed as though Marie had lived with Little Precious forever, even though it had only been a few months since she'd rescued the pup from the pound. The dog catcher had netted Precious, half-starved and abandoned, wandering through a pseudo-Swiss subdivision of abandoned, collapsing houses out by the airport. Little Precious, whose name had been Trixie in another life, had now and forever proven herself to be a giant killer, as well.

Marie Higgins made a lovely Virgin Mary. She fit perfectly under the stable roof right next to the manger. During rehearsals, she practiced gazing down at the plaster baby with a mysterious, haunting smile. Everyone found her performance enchanting.

Helen resigned herself to the role of costume coordinator. The evening of the performance, she was helping others into their robes when Coach Bear Lonnier staggered into the dressing hall. Bear had never missed a year playing Joseph and he was determined to be there, even though he'd come down with flu and raging fever.

"I'm sick as a dog," he told Helen.

Helen took control and grasped her opportunity. "The show must go on," she said.

She skinned Bear out of his robe and his fake beard, donned his costume, and played the part of Joseph. She did a fine job and never moved a muscle.

CLARA, PART ONE:
SINGLE FAMILIAR OBJECT

"All dogs dream wolf dreams, and know they're dreaming of biting their master. Every dog knows, deep in his heart, that he is a Bad Dog."
~Terry Pratchett

WE WERE DRIVING in the countryside, Eugene at the wheel, me beside him with Skippy on my lap. Lord, that dog surely loves a car ride. Eugene and I were quiet with each other the way people are after forty years. Not silence, because silence comes at you from outside. We were enjoying quiet that comes from inside, roomy and comfortable. That's where we stayed most of the time, unless something came up and we needed to discuss it, and that's what happened that day. Something came up. It came right up.

Delta farmland is flat and empty and as old as time. The air's so thick with history that sounds ride for miles on the shoulders of ghosts. We're a whisper away from the afterlife, with our haunted battlefields and mossy cemeteries. There's an unchanging permanence, so when something new appears in the countryside, it's more than shocking; it's revolutionary. The damn thing dominated the flat horizon. It was huge—gigantic, in fact—and as we moved closer, it loomed over us, towering by the side of the road, bigger than a dinosaur and as much out of place. I said to Eugene, "Look at that."

Eugene craned his neck and said, "Wow, Clara."

We pulled over and gawked, and even Skippy put his little paws on the dashboard and craned up at the enormous billboard on a single round steel leg, like a Popsicle on a stick. I believe billboards are an abomination, I certainly do. I'm grateful that St. Bernard councilmen don't allow the damn things, but here it was anyway, next to the road, a few yards inside the town line. Later, we found out that the councilmen had erected the damn thing. I guess they wanted to get a last-minute message to young people on their way into town to raise some hell. The billboard had a picture of a giant marijuana leaf inside a red circle with a red band across it, and at the bottom it said, "Dope! Don't Smoke It!"

For a long time, the councilmen had been worried about our kids and marijuana. (This was coming from middle-aged hypocrites who, in their day, raided cow pastures for mushrooms and cooked LSD in college dorm rooms.) "Oh, that'll really stop the kids from smoking, for sure," Eugene said in that sarcastic way he could put things and make them funny.

Marijuana? Hell, we were flower children of the sixties, me'n Eugene. We'd come of age in a waving sea of it. Dope fueled our dreams of a floral universe. We tried it all and saw it all, including JFK's promise—manned space flight. It was the ultimate psychedelic rush, watching Neil Armstrong step out on the moon on a snowy TV screen while we passed around a big doobie on the couch. There's not much wonder and amazement in the world today, but we made it happen back then. Everything was new and the future was rosy, even for a couple of kids from the swamplands.

Eugene said, "Yeah, kids, don't smoke it. Eat it. Those brownies are gooood!"

He started giggling and got me going too, so we drove the next few miles laughing because the councilmen didn't have a clue about what went on in the world. They thought they could make something go away by posting a twenty-foot picture of it. That billboard wasn't a deterrent; it was a giant spliff, a sales pitch, a love letter to hooch. The biggest publicity shot of all.

"Clara, that puts me in mind of the Jacksons," Eugene said.

"Ahh," I said, "Right."

Elvis and Otis Jackson were local boys, identical twins, and our unofficial village idiots. They made their living as country and western singers touring the fairground circuit, state to state, like the Everly Brothers, only more matching. Being twins, Elvis and Otis shared everything, including the same woman. She'd shown up in the audience one night, a typical stage-side groupie in a fringed leather jacket and snagged leopard leotards dented by panty lines, and she took up with Elvis and Otis in tandem. The twins looked so much alike that the woman could barely tell them apart, so after a while she stopped trying.

Eventually, after routine congress with one twin or the other, she gave birth to a son. A year later, she birthed a second son. Being deeply celebrity-crazed, she named her first-born Michael Jackson and her second-born Jesse Jackson. Nobody, including the mother, knew which twin fathered Michael and which twin fathered Jesse, but the fine points seemed to be hypothetical. They all settled into a peculiar three-parent family unit that was so bizarre it freaked out the other seasoned musicians on the music circuit, even those performers whose stock and trade was wholehearted exhibitionism.

After a few years of swinging from Elvis to Otis and back again, the Spandex groupie finally realized the difference between fertility and futility, so she abandoned the toddlers and their twin daddies. Elvis and Otis were forced to give up their music careers and settle down to raise their sons Michael and Jesse, but over the years they continued to fondly mention the joys of bonding with the audience.

When we considered the show business atmosphere of their formative years, we weren't surprised that Michael and Jesse grew up and took jobs in the public eye. I'd seen them at work, which was dancing nearly naked, so naturally I'd seen quite a bit. They were a cheap variation of Chippendale male dancers, but taken to the next level, which was the final step to which it could be taken, short of being arrested. They called themselves Chipmunks and worked up a synchronized dance, mostly sweating while thrusting to music. They wore clip-on pointy ears and snap-on tails. Their business card bore a tacky logo of a gyrating squirrel in a G-string.

At first, they played to ladies' birthday parties, bridal showers, and girl luncheons, and business flourished. Eventually bookings fell off sharply when the local ladies became saturated in what the Jackson boys had to offer. Sweaty imitation lust and clumsy dancing simply couldn't sustain genuine interest. As for their masculine attributes, we'd witnessed the organic gifts of Jesse and Michael so regularly that those parts grew commonplace. If the boys hadn't looked so much alike, they might've held more fascination, but they were too similar for any defining novelty. The exhibitionism business continued to decline, so Jesse Jackson took a job at the chicken packing plant and Michael Jackson hired on with a house roofer.

After a while, Michael's boss, the house roofer, took his family to Disney World and Michael had a few days unencumbered by shingles. Spare time had never sat easy with Michael and he tended to stray into mischief and nonsense. In practically no time at all, he stumbled across that human skeleton in the woods.

The Jackson property abutted a stretch of woods where the sheriff had recently discovered and destroyed a crop of damn fine cannabis secreted among the trees. Michael sprawled in a lawn chair in his littered yard and guzzled beer while the last of his dope smoldered between his fingers. He gazed into the woods, pondering if any of that destroyed crop was self-seeding and might've grown up wild and unclaimed. He phoned his brother Jesse at the chicken packing plant and told him to come over after work and help search the woods for weed. Jesse, being agreeable, showed up as soon as he'd packed his quota of fryers.

As Michael later told the police, he and Jesse were making their way along an animal trail when a covey of quail fluttered out of the bushes and startled them. Michael fell sideways and tumbled downhill into a soggy creek bed. He rolled over and came face to face with the empty eyeholes of a skull buried up to the cheekbones in mud. Screaming and scuttling ensued, after which he summoned the law. Michael stuck to a wide-eyed claim that he and Jesse had been bird watching in the woods, albeit without benefit of binoculars or any workable knowledge of fowl except for the fact that Jesse packed them.

Yellow caution tape was strung among the trees and the skeleton was excavated amid a mountain of paperwork. TV news reported on the bones, which meant the Jacksons were suddenly thrust into the spotlight without having to undress. They granted an interview with the press, but it only solidified the conclusion that any intelligent discovery the boys made must've been accidental.

The cops said the skeleton was probably a nameless drifter and the cause of death was pending, but the coroner wasn't ruling out foul play. Anyone with information should notify the police. I went to the phone and told the girl on the police switchboard that the coroner was too young to know local history. "If he did," I said, "he'd realize that the skeleton is probably a Koonts or a Tarbuckle. They were feuding, you know, and shooting each other in those woods."

"A feud, ma'am?" the operator drawled, "I ain't never heard of no feud."

"Of course you haven't. How old are you? Eighteen? It started with a fight over a raccoon, thirty years ago; Junior Tarbuckle's pet raccoon, Bandit Tarbuckle. The Koonts were fond of raccoons too, but preferred them on a plate with gravy. The Koonts were known to be lazy and thieves to boot, so when Bandit's cage turned up empty, the Tarbuckles figured the Koonts had stolen him and served him up with candied yams. The thought of Bandit working his way through several Koonts digestive tracts caused Junior Tarbuckle no small amount of anguish, so to get even, Junior snuck over to the Koonts farm and shot a Koonts hound dog."

"That's fine, lady," the switchboard girl said. "Thanks for calling."

"Wait! That's not all. The Koonts were fond of their dogs to an unnatural degree and bedded down with them on cold nights, so, in return, the Koonts went over and shot a Tarbuckle pig. The Tarbuckles doted on their pigs and had given them all names, so the Tarbuckles retaliated by shooting a Koonts goat. The loss of a beloved goat prompted the Koonts to execute a Tarbuckle cow, which is the largest animal either of them owned."

The switchboard girl said, "Ma'am . . . please."

"Naturally, there was nowhere to go but bigger and better, but neither clan owned an elephant, so the Tarbuckles settled for an unfortunate Koonts cousin. This led to the shooting of a Tarbuckle cousin in fair return. Since there were ample worthless cousins on both sides, the clans simply buried the unlucky cousins in the woods and neither clan reported the murders to the law. Of course, by then, both sides were much too fond of the feud to end it."

"Buried cousins in the woods, ma'am?" she asked, "I don't reckon so. I know them Koontses and Tarbuckles. I doubt they kilt any cousins."

"Well," I said, "you only know tame Koontses and Tarbuckles. They were wilder back then, with low thresholds of boredom, too much pride, and nothing to be proud of. Tell the coroner to compare the skeleton DNA with samples from both families, if they've finally evolved to the point where they actually have DNA."

She scraped up the grace to thank me for my input and again attempted to hang up, made hums and hahs, but I wasn't through with the disrespectful smart-ass. "Hold on a minute. Better to be buried in the woods," I told the little twit, "than to die shut up in your house, rotting away undiscovered and smelling to high heaven."

She agreed with me and redoubled her effort to cut me off.

I said, "Junior Tarbuckle was so deconstructed by the loss of Bandit that he turned to a life of crime. He was the first outlaw to plant a fine crop of weed in the woods where the dirt was enriched, I suspect, by all the buried cousins. Luckily, Junior had a green thumb and both Koontses and Tarbuckles harvested dope until they were so laid-back that they forgave each other, except for Junior who refused to put Bandit behind him. He dropped out of the world and smoked himself to death with his own product, alone in his house, quite mellowed out."

The switchboard girl said something like well thanks and goodbye.

I said, "Dead two weeks before they found him, alerted by the stink. When they picked Junior up, their fingers went right through his rotten skin, just like punching through an overripe tomato. They brought his swollen, leaky remains out in a giant zip-lock bag."

"Bye, lady," she said, her voice quivering.

I paused to light a cigarette, drawing out the time like the actress Bette Davis. Bette knew a few things about timing. That's why Bette always smoked in her movies. Each puff was an elegant pause, a three-count. I blew a smoke ring and said "Windows of his house were black with flies. Can you imagine the smell?"

The little switchboard bitch was silent now, defeated.

I finished, "But that was Junior Tarbuckle, a rotten old toker to the end."

The phone clicked and hummed.

"Ahh," I said, smiling.

THE SKELETON FOUND by Michael and Jesse Jackson had been unearthed because the four elements—wind, water, earth, and fire—don't combine very well in the Delta where we live. Those elements are always at war, and it skews everything a little bit off the natural plane. Winds howl across our fields, shearing off layers of topsoil, fanning wildfires and spreading sparks. Soil and water are at odds, too, like alien life forms thrown together. We had torrents of rain that spring, and great sections of wet earth began to move. The topsoil melted into a wide river of mud sliding slowly through lowlands and down Michael Jackson's creek bed, groaning like a beast, knocking over everything in its path and bringing that skeleton along for the ride. That's my opinion, but I've lived a long time on this odd, spongy soil, and I've seen things get up and move, even after they've been properly buried.

Michael and Jesse never found the wild weed they were seeking that spring, but their luck changed with the coming of summer. The spring rains tapered off and the earth stopped sliding and our woods exploded in rich, vibrant, self-seeding summer green which must've included marijuana because the Jacksons showed up in town with a supply of freshly harvested weed and were promptly arrested. The judge gave them six months of picking up roadside litter, as a method of educating them. Eugene and I passed the boys on the side of the road many times. We laughed and honked, and they smiled and waved and kept on cleaning up trash, but I doubt they learned anything.

Some things can't be taught. Once, Eugene gave me an empty bird nest he'd found. He said, "Clara, I got two hands and I couldn't create this amazing thing and I sure as hell couldn't make it with my pecker, like the bird did." Simple creatures often do complex things, but some complex creatures can't even learn the simplest of things. The Jackson boys would never walk a straight line down the middle. Their feet didn't move that way.

The skeleton Michael found was never identified. Guess there wasn't enough human DNA in the Koontses and Tarbuckles to lay kin. The bones couldn't be buried because the case was still under investigation, so the coroner stored the bones in a drawer, hoping the future might shed some light.

I told Eugene, "I feel bad about those bones. No matter what happened to that cousin, the poor soul deserves to rest in peace, but now his bones are sitting in the coroner's drawers."

Eugene said, "Not really, Clara. It doesn't matter what happens to his bones because his spirit's moved on. He's walking strange territory now, waiting for the rest of us to catch up. We'll all get there eventually, because we're just cosmic travelers in time and space. Space isn't such a bad place to be."

My gray-haired flower child waltzed me around the living room like he did sometimes, singing our special song, "Moon River." He knew all the words. Skippy yipped and danced around our feet and we had to shuffle, catching each other, to keep from stepping on him. "One small step for man," Eugene laughed, and scooped up the dog. "Clara darling, let's fly to the moon!"

"Oh no, Eugene. I'd be too scared."

"Everybody's scared, Clara, all the time. Strange territory always terrifies us. We just shut the door on it and go on living." He laughed at the doubt on my face. "Courage is simply ignoring what's on the other side of the door. Come on, Clara, or you'll miss out. The moon's the greatest show spinning in the heavens."

He held Skippy in one arm and me in the other, and the three of us spun around and around. Then, he sat down, panting. "Chest hurts," he said.

The next day, Eugene died.

That was the day that our shared quiet ended and my isolated silence began. My ears ring with it. I hurt, and that hurt is forever collapsing inward with sharp edges. Our old local landmarks are shuffled. I'm disoriented. The familiar is indifferent. I keep forgetting what comes next. I have a new understanding of the word *constant*. Eugene's under my skin like the watermark on stationery. Nothing washes off. It can't be shrugged away.

I need the courage Eugene talked about. Not enough courage

to go to the moon, just enough to stay here on earth without him. Native Americans hereabouts say that grief leaves us through our mouths. We have to talk it away, but those hated words hurt me, cutting me on the way out, so I push them down and keep them behind my throat, below my eyes. I don't have the courage to say them. Not yet.

Eugene is somewhere else now, in strange territory, branching out. He's still here too, in spinning eddies of air, as though he just brushed past me. He is constant.

When astronauts become disoriented in space, they're taught to focus their thoughts on a single familiar object; a fishing hat or coffee cup, a soft tee shirt, something well known and constant. They find their equilibrium this way. So I sit on the porch at night and scan the heavens looking for—what? A familiar object? Well, why not? Plenty of familiar constellations. I tip up my chin and starlight falls into my eyes. Eugene was right when he said that space isn't such a bad destination, once you master the concept of neverending.

I see pinpoints of light, diamonds on a black blanket, spheres of erupting mystery . . . expanding . . . hypnotic. The stars are slowly dying, every single one, but even when their end comes, we won't know it because the light that reaches us was sent out millions of years ago. In our brief time, the stars will always seem forever constant, the place where all creation began, serving us, each to our own heart's purpose.

Reflecting in a lover's eyes.

Shaping an astronomer's constellations.

Guiding a sailor home through troubled seas.

Granting a dreamer's wish.

My sweet Eugene, some nights I dream of an Arctic glacier. Miles down in the glacier is a layer of snow that fell forty years ago, on the same night you first took me to bed. The earth would have to be destroyed in a rain of fire before that deep layer evaporated, but if I were still around to breathe the mist of that ice, with my last breath I couldn't give up the joy of that night with you. There should've been only a faint memory, or at least embarrassment, but the remembrance is there, sensual and sharp as if it had happened yesterday.

Wrapped in a dream of ice, we are warm.

We are constant.

CLARA, PART TWO:
LAST GLEAMING

> "Why do dogs make one want to cry?
> There is something so quiet and
> hopeless about their sympathy."
> ~Daphne Du Maurier

HERE, THEN, IS a muffled world in dripping suspension. Misty rain, sky the color of an aluminum washtub, no birdsong, no cars passing, nobody. On closer look, there's meager movement. An old woman, Clara in Eugene's oversize galoshes. She wades slowly through standing water. . . schlop . . . schlop . . . down her driveway toward the back door. Clara's much more stooped these past few months.

Eyes down, she sees a metal sky reflected in puddles; sees her neglected lawn, shabby along the edges of the concrete where prodding tendrils of yellow centipede snake onto the pavement. Eugene never tolerated a shaggy lawn, but he's been gone for months. Seasons have passed, and he's still dead.

Didn't come back, no, no.

The Britt boy cuts her yard for money, shitty little thug. He says he trims the grass along the concrete edges, but he doesn't. Not an inch. He thinks she's old and won't notice. He takes her money with a grin, without conscience.

"Ahh," Clara says, when she sees the shaggy edges.

Let the boy spend her money, he can't buy his way out of being a liar. It's only grass, trying to grow and spread. Holding grass back seems unnatural to her, always did. It was Eugene who thought that nature could be disciplined.

Her house needs paint, but paint's unnatural too, covering the beauty of wood with a coat of phony color that flakes away in the sun, some garish shade of the Caribbean, in this place, nowhere near

Jamaica.

Oh Jamaica, where they never worry about the next meal. Plenty of food in their trees, in their nets, they've no need to be intense, those gentle ocean grazers, laughing and barefoot, prying open oysters on the beach. Clara's seen the Gulf a few times, but didn't like it. She likes easy oysters from the supermarket, slick in a plastic tub, floating in cloudy brine.

Sometimes her thoughts spin beyond control. She knows her words are hazy and unreasonable, even as she says them, but she throws them out like anchors at the end of long ropes. She says any inane or shocking thing to preserve her importance so others can't ignore her. She knows she's pure and wise; her words have weight, so she says them, and it's as though a breeze has drifted past, no substance, no snagging anchors. In the ache of her loneliness, she wraps herself in a silent pout and the silence rings.

Ah, here's her back door, where it ever was.

She's forgetful since Eugene died; forgets where she needs to go, or the day of the week, or where she put something, but she can still make her way to this door with the conviction of a spawning salmon. Purse over her arm, she shifts her umbrella to grip the handrail and she sees it, a tan-colored blob on the ground under her dripping rose bush.

What the hell . . . ?

She uses the umbrella to lean upon, to tilt a line of sight through the leaves. He comes into focus, her ancient little dog Skippy, wet and dead against the root crown. He must be dead; he wouldn't tolerate such a soaking, otherwise.

"Skippy, oh Skippy, come here, boy!" she calls.

No response. Just the wet rose bush, dripping. Wet ground. Wet dog, unmoving.

Clara straightens and blinks. "Ahh."

She's swamped by immediate sorrow, bewilderment, piercing loneliness, not in a mature fashion, but disorienting and alien, as a child might experience it. There are things she should do now, with this discovery. The dead always leave us with chores. There'll be cleaning up, words to invent, the work involved in a proper funeral, be it man or beast or sodden, aged dog. She lived with Skippy many years, longer than she lived with a lot of things, except Eugene. Now, there's only this chore, this enormous task, in the way.

She briefly considers wrapping Skippy in newspaper as though he were a dead fish and storing him in the freezer until the Britt boy, the little cheater, can dig a hole, which is not a bad idea. But like a ripple on a pond, the plan moves smoothly to the edge of her mind and bumps against a stubborn shore of resistance. The kid is a rotten apple, a mean little shit. He hated Skippy, and the sentiment was mutual. Skippy barked at him, an unyielding yip-yip. Once, she watched through the window as the boy kick the dog. Another time he swung a rake, making Skippy howl with pain.

Even more than the little thug's meanness, she can't stand the idea of her Skippy wrapped in newspaper, stiff and frosty in the freezer while she eats her supper alone at the kitchen table nearby.

Eugene spoke of the olden days, when bodies of dead Vikings were burned to ashes. She may not be able to dig a grave, but she can still build a fire, so why not?

It's decided; cremation, the ancient Viking way, the funeral pyre, on a raised platform between heaven and earth. Skippy liked warm places. He slept on the heated bricks of the fireplace on cold days.

She'll need a proper location and a hot fire to do the job. Eugene had built a cooking fire, two years ago or more, burning meat on a cheap crusted grill. The grill was red and rounded on the bottom like half a cracked egg, lidless, with rubber wheels. As far as she remembers, that grill's still around, rusting in her potting shed. The open area behind the shed would make a good setting for the funeral pyre, near the compost heap, so she could simply tip Skippy's ashes into the compost to be spread upon her flowers. The little thug will spread Skippy around and never realize it, and Skippy won't mind. She scooped his dung for years and tossed it into the flowerbeds as fertilizer. No freezer for Skippy then, no crook's hole in the ground. Her loving companion will nourish the flowers, the roses. A comforting notion.

She stands in the yard, drizzle soaked, rubbing her wet forehead with age-misshapen fingers. There should be procedure; there must be combustible fuel, at least at first, to ignite the body. That stack of yellowed newspapers in the shed will do nicely. Dry, brittle newsprint, fuel enough for a little pup. She hooks her umbrella and purse over the handrail of the back steps.

She's thirsty, always favors a beer in the afternoons, looks forward to it on the walk home. She often takes a few shots of good Russian vodka, a community cup of sorts, because she shared it with Eugene with a bit of ceremony and juice. Now it gives her solace almost every day.

She goes to the potting shed, pulls open the scraping door, rotten at the bottom. Ahhh, there's the grill. She stacks dusty newspapers on the grid and rolls it to the open space behind the shed, beside the compost heap. The grill is shaky, so she braces it against the shed's back wall and covers the grid with a thick layer of newsprint. Then, it's back to the rosebush, back to Skippy.

The body is deep beneath thorny limbs, so she uses the hooked handle of her umbrella to snag his collar and pull him out. Skippy slides on mud, surprisingly weightless, and his lightness twists her heart with guilt. When had he become so thin and frail?

She plucks a couple of roses and shoves the blooms into her pocket and begins to pull the dog behind her. She whimpers as Skippy bumps along, sodden and limp and open-eyed, with the tip of his pink tongue protruding. It takes both hands and all her strength to lift and lever the umbrella high enough to unhook Skippy awkwardly above the newspapers. He drops with a thud upon the classifieds. She shreds the roses and scatters pedals over him, sobbing now, recalling Skippy napping in her lap, snoring softly, his pink belly warming her wasted thighs.

"Skippy, you're a bit soaked, so you may be hard to light." Her quivering voice, the sudden sobbing breath, surprise her. "I have to find some fuel, boy."

She searches the garage for charcoal lighter, preoccupied and sobbing less now, brushing at her wet eyes. Eugene probably used it all and didn't replace it. Not replacing, leaving her stranded, one of his bad habits.

"Ahh," she growls, and puts her face in her hands.

Eugene had laughed so hard every time Skippy stood, hind legs in Eugene's lap, front legs on Eugene's collar bones, bumping Eugene's wrinkled face with a wet nose, dog Eskimo kisses. Clara suspends her search and hauls herself up the back steps to have a shot of vodka. She keeps a bottle in the freezer, where she refuses to put Skippy. The cap unscrews with an effort. She pours two fingers of vodka into a jelly glass, lifts it and sips. The familiar distraction of heat. "Ahh."

She looks over her pantry for something flammable to boost the cremation, turns and sees the vodka bottle on the counter. She takes it in her hand uncapped, finds the matches in a drawer, teeters outside.

"Here Skippy, my friend. Let's share this."

She douses him with cold vodka. After several arthritic attempts, she strikes a long match, holds it aloft. All hymns of her childhood escape her, so she hums "The Star Spangled Banner" as she touches the match to Skippy. Vodka flares like a torch. Flames shoot up five feet as fire quickly leaps to the potting shed. The old porous wood expands with a *whomp* and a sudden expulsion of air as the shed's back wall ignites.

"Bad dog! Just look what you've done!"

Clara backs away from the heat and shuffles toward the house to make an emergency call; almost yells for Eugene in her confusion. On the way, she stops to catch her breath, until the crackle of burning wood and smell of charring dog remind her to hurry. "Ahh," she says in frustration, hits her forehead with the heel of her hand as she climbs the steps and goes into the house.

Eugene had posted the number for the fire department, but she can't find it, so she calls 911 and explains that her dog has set fire to the potting shed. The dispatcher asks if she's sure about that.

"Oh, yes, dear. And he smells damn awful too, you know— burning fur. I basted him in vodka."

The dispatcher suppresses a surge of nausea. *"What?"*

"Well, hell, he was too wet to light, and you can't cremate a dog that won't light."

The dispatcher, fully repulsed, sets the mechanism of response into action. Her report dutifully includes dog and vodka.

Hook and ladder and pumper trucks pull up in front. Fat white water hoses soon criss-cross the street. A fireman named Charlie LaForce, whose dog Lucky Jack can talk when he pleases, is on duty that afternoon.

"What cause dis fire?" Charlie asks another fireman.

The other fireman answers, "That old lady was trying to cremate a dog."

Charlie asks, "Was the dog dead?"

"Jesus, I hope so."

Clara taps Charlie LaForce on the shoulder. "Are you a fireman?"

Charlie turns. "Beg pardon, ma'am?"

"Are you a fireman?"

Charlie grins. "Me? Yessum, most certainly am."

"Skippy died. He's on the barbecue grill. Can you put his ashes in my compost heap? I want that little bastard to put him on my roses."

"Sure can, ma'am, now would you go on the porch where it safe so we can put out dis fire?"

"Okay, but I'm keeping an eye on you. Tend to those dog ashes, you hear?"

Firemen feed hoses onto the property. One of the men says, "Seems like she would've buried the dog. Old people love funerals."

Charlie, grins. "Who need a pet cem'tery when dere's a barbecue grill?"

Clara yells at him from the porch, "What are you laughing at? I'm watching you!"

The potting shed is extinguished and rendered to a dripping shell. Charlie approaches Clara on the porch. "Ma'am, we found your dog. He still whole, no ashes. What we do wit him?"

"There's still something of him left?"

"Yessum. You burnt mostly shed, vodka, and fur. Dere still more dog'n you would imagine, given what he been through."

"You boys got a shovel?"

"We gotta buncha shovels, jes not much time." Then, Charlie softens. "Where you want the hole dug?"

Clara, smudged and sooty, ashes in her white hair, picks a spot and Charlie digs a hasty hole under her supervision. He summons the other firemen and they assemble around the grave as he lowers

Skippy with the shovel, fills the shallow grave, and pats the mound with the back of the spade.

Clara glares at Charlie expectantly, as though he should say a few words of comfort. He glances at the other fireman, sighs, and begins, "Lord, please take—"

Clara interrupts, launching into an off-key National Anthem. Firemen snatch their helmets from their heads and hold them over their hearts. Clara finishes: . . . *homer the braaaavveee* . . . holding the last note for a surprisingly long time. Without a word she turns and goes into the house, slamming the door. The firemen shrug, load up, and drive away.

THAT EVENING, CLARA steps out on the back porch, beer in hand, and almost calls for Skippy, but then she sees the remains of the shed and remembers. She bumps her forehead with her hand. "Ahh."

Clara tips her chin to look at the stars, dependable constellations from the beginning of time. A soft night breeze touches her lined face. She flutters pink-rimmed eyes. The scent of a recent wood fire drifts from the shell of the potting shed. Such a comforting smell, a primeval reminder of warmth, light, food, companions. Clara smiles in response, bends and carefully lowers her backside to the step as she did when Eugene was there to sit beside her, when Skippy dozed at her feet.

"Eugene, I almost forgot. Skippy's with you now."

The sultry night wraps her like a shawl. She's comforted by the familiarity of her own backyard, and she relaxes into trickles of silent tears. The human soul, a cup of sadness. Clara's soul must be almost full by now. *Dear God, it has to be*, she thinks and clears her wet eyes with the back of her hand.

She talks to the scraps of Eugene she can see . . . his lawn, his flowerbeds. Her voice dissolves into the warm evening air like sugar in tea. "I'm leaving this old world, a slow piece at a time, Eugene, yet I wake up every day, still here. I'm tired of loneliness, and . . .and . . . I'm so pissed at you all the time for leaving me. It's embarrassing, Eugene, being the last one, still here, like I have nowhere to go, like

I don't know how to leave. Why can't I be with you and Skippy, like we used to be?"

No reply, only crickets, those night chirpers, and a flutter of moths at the porch light. Clara looks at the tipping cups of the big and little dippers. At the edge of her vision, the fiery August star Sirius flickers and burns. Stars are untainted by eras; they spin in peace and endless time; origins of light in the cold ether of space. As with Eugene and Skippy, they're pure mystery now.

Her memories are clear and dramatic. She's a sum, the total of his years plus her years braided like a rope, a lifeline. The cadence of a waltz begins to throb, softly at first, then unfolding in a pulsing orchestra of memories. Violins swell and surge, a stream of rhythm. Moon River, Eugene knew all the words. Humming the melody, she sets down her beer and rises on shaky legs, lifts a twisted hand to the heavens, and waves.

Photo: Ben Mayer

Pat Mayer is a native of Alabama. She is the author of the novels *Terminal Bend* and *The Cannibals Said Grace*. She has twice been nominated for the Pushcart Prize and was awarded first place in the 2007 International Limerick competition. She and her husband Paul live in Mobile.